SPARROWS

Ann Aschauer

Sparrows

ISBN: 978-1-60920-023-7
Printed in the United States of America
©2011 by Ann Aschauer
All rights reserved

Cover and interior design by Ajoyin Publishing, Inc.

Library of Congress Control Number: 2011927498

All scripture quotations, unless otherwise indicated, are taken from the Holy Bible, International Version®, NIV®. Copyright ©1973, 1978, 1984, 2011 by Biblica, Inc.™ Used by permission of Zondervan. All rights reserved worldwide. www.zondervan.com

API
Ajoyin Publishing, Inc.
P.O. 342
Three Rivers, MI 49093
www.ajoyin.com

Please direct your inquiries to admin@ajoyin.com

SPARROWS

Ann Aschauer

Ajoyin Publishing, Inc.
PO Box 342
Three Rivers, MI 49093
1.888.273.4JOY
www.ajoyin.com

DEDICATION

To my grandchildren: May you rise up as children of God to be a powerful force for His kingdom in your generation. (It's OK, you'll know what all that means in a decade or so.)

Tim and Mary Ann: Thank you so much for all your help, encouragement, and hospitality when I was doing my research.

Pam and Sherry: It's so great having publishers that are sisters in the Lord. I've enjoyed the good fellowship of our "business meetings." Thanks for all your ideas, support, and most of all your prayers.

Above all, Jesus: You know all my flaws and use me anyway. Thank You for Your grace and patience with me, and for letting me be a part of Your plan.

PART I

"For my thoughts are not your thoughts,
neither are your ways my ways," declares the LORD.
"As the heavens are higher than the earth,
so are my ways higher than your ways
and my thoughts than your thoughts."

—Isaiah 55:8-9

February 28, 2007

Abdul awoke while it was still dark. He checked the time and found that it was just moments before the alarm was to go off. He hit the button to preserve the quiet in his hotel room. The first call to prayer was in a half hour, and he wanted to be sure to have completed all the rituals necessary for his prayers to be effective. Although the *wudu*, or lesser ablution was sufficient for him most mornings, he allowed himself time for the full *ghusl*; he wanted to be absolutely sure he was purified this morning.

When the ritual had been completed, his mouth and nostrils rinsed and his entire body washed according to the prescribed rules, Abdul put on his clean robe for the pre-dawn prayer.

Soon he heard the mournful-sounding wail of the call to prayer echoing through the city and dutifully took his position to pray, facing Mecca. His heart leapt; today was *the day*.

He had not yet become accustomed to thinking of himself as a martyr. He had never felt quite worthy of the title; such an honor had seemed more fitting for his older brother Mohammed. Yet here he was, the chosen one to carry out this chapter of *jihad*.

The prayers he recited were the usual ones, the same ones spoken by Muslims all over the world, yet this morning they had a special feel to them. With a sense of wonder Abdul realized that while this morning he was in Jerusalem, saying his prayers, tonight he would be in Paradise, with seventy-two virgins at his beckon call.

He was still thinking about them as he splashed on cologne—a little more cologne than usual. Although he knew it would be the virgins' duty to please him, he hoped, in a Western-type surge of sentimentality, that he would please them, too. He didn't know if things such as a fragrance would survive the blast that would send his soul into the hereafter, but he felt it was worth a try, anyway. He paused for a moment before the mirror that reflected an insecure young man. He gazed critically at the dark eyes, round face, and black hair with auburn highlights that had always seemed unkempt, even moments after he had combed it. When he was a child his mother had always fussed over his disheveled appearance. She never said so, but Abdul felt she and his father had preferred Mohammed, their eldest son. He was the one who had always made them proud, and who had taken over the responsibilities as man of the house after Father had died in battle.

But today Abdul would be the hero. This was *his* moment of glory. Today his mother would learn of his martyrdom, and at last she would be proud of her younger son, maybe even more than of the older, more handsome Mohammed. Father would have been proud as well. After all, what were good looks compared to the glory of *jihad* and the status of martyr? And he felt sure, or at least he hoped, that his martyrdom would make him irresistible to his virgins.

Abdul carefully strapped on the explosive devices, seeing to it that everything was properly connected and ready to detonate at the appointed moment. He checked and rechecked down to the last detail, wanting to be doubly sure nothing would go wrong. When the devices were set and lying as flat as possible against his skin, he covered them with his clean white tunic and outer garment, making sure the detonation button was hidden yet within reach. As Abdul inspected himself in the mirror, he checked every angle to make sure nothing was conspicuous. Finally, when he was satisfied that he was prepared for the task at hand, he set out from the hotel room.

As he stepped off the elevator, the smells of breakfast came wafting through the lobby. He resisted the temptation to indulge in one last meal before his martyrdom; he would be in Paradise soon enough, with untold delights that no doubt would make any earthly feast seem pitiful in comparison.

As he made his way down the street, past shop-owners, tourists, journalists, soldiers, and police, he was seized with the irrational fear that everyone he passed knew exactly what he was up to, yet they walked by without giving him a second glance. He tried by sheer will power to steady the pounding of his heart, lest someone see its palpitations through his clothes.

Arriving at the bus stop, he tried to look casual, but realizing he was early, he decided to cross the street and buy a paper at the news stand.

The headlines were of little interest to him as he leaned against the building, pretending to be reading. He stole an occasional glance over the top of the paper as he turned the pages every few moments and took note when the first Israeli boys began to congregate at the bus stop. They ranged in age from about six to about twelve, some of the smaller ones holding the hands of their older brothers. Their faces were scrubbed, their hair was combed, and rosy cheeks seemed as much a part of their uniform as the black pants and white starched shirts. They drifted in from different directions, giving each other routine greetings.

Finally, when there were about a dozen of them, Abdul knew the moment was close. He watched the end of the block out of the corner of his eye, and when he spotted the school bus rounding the corner, he casually folded his paper and stood waiting for the crossing signal to change. His hands fidgeted nervously. The light seemed to be taking forever, and he could see the children beginning to board the bus.

The moment the signal changed he walked briskly to the other side, arriving just as the last boy stood in the doorway of the bus.

Perfect timing! he thought. *Praise be to Allah!* In one swift move, he stepped onto the bus after the child, and his eyes met those of the startled driver. Reaching into his garment for the detonation device, Abdul faced the busload of young faces, all eyes on him, some frightened, some puzzled, some curious. A momentary notion of their innocence lighted in his mind like a timid butterfly, which was immediately whisked away with the thought that took the form of one word: *Infidels.*

Before anyone had a chance to react, Abdul pressed the button.

Immediately there was a flash of light, a deafening explosion, and a hint of pain that quickly turned into a sort of numbness and a sense of weightlessness. Abdul could hear screams in the street that sounded very distant and quickly faded into silence.

He was surprised at how easy it had been—so much easier than all the preparation and anticipation, all the misgivings and haunting notions of everything that could go wrong. It had all gone just as planned, and he was on his way to Paradise, with nothing fearsome or unpleasant ever to have to endure again.

The floating sensation enveloped him, and bright colors began to glisten in vague shapes and patterns. Sounds like distant music came on a warm breeze that caressed his skin and carried delicious, inviting aromas.

Paradise was coming into focus, and it overwhelmed all of his senses. Abdul had never seen anything more beautiful; it was more than his earthly eyes ever could have taken in all at once—the mountains, the streams, the islands, the gardens, the waterfalls, the heavens strewn with stars, rainbows, sunsets, and flocks of white birds.

The music was inexpressibly beautiful as well. It sounded like a multitude of instruments—familiar, yet unidentified—what must have been millions of strings, trumpets singing out from everywhere simultaneously; even the thunder had a musical quality to it. Every delightful fragrance seemed present at once, yet they did not clash but blended in perfect, sensual harmony. He could see trees with ripening fruit adorning the landscape, and at the base of the closest one were several brightly-colored cushions inviting him to come and rest.

Abdul stood in awe, scarcely able to take it all in. He sat on the cushions and dangled his fingers in a small pool. The ripples in the water sent beams of light in all directions, each one carrying with it an indescribable melody that gave him a sensation that was like every pleasure at once; it was warm, cool, soft, relaxing, invigorating.

Then he saw them. They stood at a respectful distance, their filmy gowns fluttering in the breeze and clinging to their young virgin bodies. Dark eyes—some shy, some flirtatious, some seductive—gazed at him over the veils that concealed the rest of their faces. Abdul's heart was racing with desire as the first one approached him, waves of jet-black hair flowing behind her and a mysterious perfume filling the air. She carried a tray with a golden goblet and a platter of every one of his favorite delicacies.

She knelt beside him, set the tray down, and laid a soft hand on his shoulder; he placed his hand over it and gave her a trembling smile. A light, musical laugh came from behind the veil as the damsel ran her fingers through his hair. A chill went through him as he thought, *So this is how I will spend eternity.*

Her face came close to his, her veil blowing aside to reveal full, red lips poised to meet his. Abdul closed his eyes in ecstatic anticipation, breathing deeply the perfume that smelled … like …

Sulfur.

Abdul was suddenly gripped with a different sensation. Something was terribly wrong, and for a moment he did not open his eyes. Whether he could not, or simply did not want to, who knew? The soft hand seemed to shrivel and harden. Claws were digging into his shoulder, and when at last he pried open his eyes, he found he was staring into the very face of Evil.

Yellow eyes—huge orbs with narrow black pupils—stared back at him in amusement. He tried to jump up but found that his feet were chained to the tree, now a gnarled, dead shell swarming with vermin; the cushions had turned to thorn bushes, the food on the tray to garbage. The musical laughter became more and more raspy and cynical. It echoed all around him, as Paradise was melting away. Trees died, flowers wilted, waterfalls ceased, and pools dried up all in a matter of moments. The mosses and grass disappeared from the hills, revealing stark, barren rock; stars and planets fell, leaving nothing but black emptiness expanding from one end of the sky to the other. Colors faded until the rainbows were gone. The white doves morphed into bats and flocked to the dead tree, eyeing Abdul threateningly. His eyes scanned the landscape for something to give him hope, and to his horror, the "virgins" were being transformed like figures in a wax museum on fire. All the delicate features were melting away, revealing scaly skin, razor-sharp teeth, long, curved talons, piercing yellow eyes, and huge nostrils that breathed foul-smelling gases. Their demonic laughter filled the air, growing louder and louder until it was piercing Abdul's ears.

"NO!" he screamed in futile protest, but these creatures clearly didn't care what he felt or wanted, any more than he had cared about the children he had so zealously murdered. The monsters were crawling toward him with the look of ravenous beasts, drooling putrid slime, surrounding him so that there was no escape. Cackling, snarling, clawing at him, they tore at his flesh in an excruciating feeding frenzy, but though Abdul expected to pass out from the pain at any moment, he didn't. The agony just continued to grow, and every moment he felt he could stand no more. Yet more would come. And the thought again occurred to him: *So this is how I will spend eternity.*

Then behind the creatures he saw a faint red glow in the sky. As it grew brighter, he saw a silhouette becoming clear. It was the shadow of a cross—the symbol of Isa, or "Jesus"—the symbol that meant so much to those misguided souls who had considered him divine. Abdul had been taught all his life to hate those people and their deifying a prophet, making him equal to Allah. To look at this symbol of their heresy, even to think about it, had seemed like an act of infidelity. But now, surrounded by demons and consumed with despair, Abdul abandoned all loyalty to Islam. He had never spoken directly to this person he had considered just one of many prophets, certainly had never prayed to him. But from somewhere deep inside his soul, he now let out a last desperate cry.

"Isa! Help me! Please!"

A hand was reaching out to him, a hand with a gaping wound in it from which blood flowed freely. It occurred to Abdul that this person may have suffered even more than he had, and yet he grasped the wounded hand as if his eternal existence depended upon it …

Abdul sat up in bed with a gasp, his body shaking and drenched with a cold sweat, his heart pounding as if it would burst. The alarm was signaling him to get up and prepare for the predawn prayer, but somehow he didn't feel like responding to it today. Instead, he lay in bed, staring into the darkness.

He knew the explosive devices were in the drawer with his clothes. He knew this was the day he was expected to carry out his mission for the cause of *jihad*. But he also knew this was the last thing he wanted to do. To a Muslim, dreams were not to be ignored. He didn't know why he kept having this one, but clearly there was a possibility that the "Paradise" he had always heard about was not all it was reputed to be.

Today he was going to have to choose whether to believe his life-long teachers or his dreams and gut feelings that were now screaming to him at full volume. It didn't take him long to decide.

He didn't know how he was going to get out of the mission. He didn't know what Hamas would do to him if they caught up to him.

He also didn't know that somewhere in America, someone was praying for him.

Five and a half years earlier …

CHAPTER ONE

"I need more ammo!" Douglas shrieked as he dived for cover behind the nearest rock.

Hunter scrambled out of the bushes and across an open area, trying hard to get to him without being hit. Unfortunately he was under heavy fire himself, and just as he reached Douglas he stumbled and fell headlong, spilling half the ammunition onto the ground. It was hardly his fault. After all, Hunter was only three, and the open bag of peas was a little too much for him to carry by himself.

"'s OK, buddy," Douglas reassured him, helping him to his feet. "Here, let's just take a few of these ... " He reloaded the peashooter and handed it to the toddler before filling his own with about a dozen of the "green bullets."

"Ready, private?"

"Ready, Unca Doug!"

"OK, here we go—*CHAAAAAARGE!*"

The two emerged, blowing hard and shooting mercilessly at "Unca Bobby" and Hunter's five-year-old sister, Lilly. Lilly screamed and ran to hide behind her uncle, while Bobby, who had been reloading himself, let loose a stream of peas at his older brother.

"Ow!" cried Doug, who had been hit hard in the ear. "Get 'im, Hunter!" Hunter, who was out of ammo, resorted to tackling Bobby. It was only because Bobby was laughing so hard and because Lilly had simultaneously grabbed him from behind that the twenty-year-old succumbed to the two toddlers and tumbled to the ground, where they proceeded to torture him with tickles until he gasped for mercy. Douglas was busy reloading the peashooters and wasn't about to come to his brother's aid anyway.

Fortunately for Bobby, his sister intervened.

"Lilly! Hunter! Y'all stop tormentin' your Unca Bobby!" Amanda scolded through the screen door. "It's time for your baths, anyway. C'mon inside now."

The response was a predictable "Aw, Mama!" as the children reluctantly relinquished their prey and headed for the door.

"Whew! Thanks, sis!" called Bobby. "I owe you one."

"Don't be too happy about it, guys. Mama wants y'all to help her some more." The young men groaned.

"Again?"

"Hey, I've been helpin' her all mornin', while *y'all* been playin' around … but thanks for keepin' the kids busy," she added with a grin. "Hey, kids, get away from that cookie jar!" She quickly disappeared from the door, but the voice of another Southern lady could be heard at the kitchen window.

"Douglas! Bobby! I need you boys to finish weedin' those flower beds now."

"The weddin's not for two weeks, Mama. Won't the weeds be back by then?"

"It's in twelve days, and if the weeds come back you can pull them again. Just keep the garden from turnin' into a jungle, please."

"Jungles are cool, Mama!" Bobby protested kiddingly.

"Bobby, please." The stress in Ellen's voice told him his mother had had enough playing around. "We really need to keep things under control. Remember," she added with a quiver in her voice, "there's one less of us now."

The brothers instantly sobered at the last plea.

"Come on, Bobby," said Douglas. "Let's go help Mama."

Since their father's death the year before, Douglas and Bobby had found it relatively easy to take over the roles of instigators of zaniness. (Their sister Amanda was a mother now, so she was somewhat handicapped, having to be the voice of reason.) But "the boys" were also now the men of the house, at least when they were home from college, and they were still getting used to the fact that their mother needed their help more than before. Things like peashooter wars kept them from dwelling on the sad fact that their father, Owen ("Jack") Jackson, was no longer with them; in fact, the wilder and more childish the activity, the more it seemed that Daddy was there in spirit. But sooner or later one needs to put the toys away and get to work, even at a summer home—especially at a summer home.

This summer the reason for Ellen's obsession with the perfect house and garden was her niece Liz's wedding. Liz and her fiancé Sean had ditched the idea of a typical wedding in St. Louis with a reception at the country club and opted for a beach wedding in northern Michigan. Ellen, whose summer home had the most room, had offered her yard for a reception by the water and under the stars—or so they hoped. The Jacksons' yard was big enough to set up a large tent, provided the volleyball net and croquet set were removed. Surrounding the property on three sides were birch trees and tall pines. The front of the house looked out onto a small lake that was connected to Lake Michigan by a channel, where in the summer one could watch the sunset between the lighthouses at the ends of two piers. All summer the lake was teeming with boats of all kinds; the sailboats were especially picturesque. Sometimes a family of swans could be seen leisurely swimming by. The setting was exquisite—or would be, as soon as the hedges were trimmed, flower beds weeded, roses pruned, shutters painted, windows washed, house painted, and grass cut one more time.

CHAPTER TWO

September 5, 2001

"Sophie did *what?!*" Liz couldn't believe what she was hearing. Surely this was one of her surreal dreams, and she would wake up any minute.

"Cancelled!" Rachel repeated; obviously the mother-of-the-bride was as stressed as the bride-to-be. "She's had a death in the family. I guess it couldn't be helped, and you can't blame her, but … "

Liz knew her mother was trying hard to refrain from saying "I told you so." … again. From the very beginning Rachel had wanted to have her daughter's wedding the "normal" way—at least "normal" for upper class St. Louis society: a big wedding at their church in Ladue followed by a reception at the country club. It was what everyone expected, but being drama-types recently graduated from the theater department, Liz and Sean were not about to settle for the usual. They had created their own scenario of a truly unique wedding on the sandy shores of Lake Michigan at sunset with Liz's friend Sophie on the harp. They would be surrounded by their most devoted friends, devoted enough to go the distance—literally—and the family's summer acquaintances that "happened to be" still be in the resort town that weekend. They had chosen the weekend after Labor Day, when the crowds of summer residents and tourists had gone home but the weather would still be beautiful, or so they hoped and prayed.

"So what do we do now?" Liz asked. It was not an expression of anger but a cry for help. Rachel took a deep breath, collected herself, and got down to business.

"Well, your cousin Susan plays the harp," she began, thinking out loud. "But … "

"But she's coming from Arizona, and a harp isn't exactly something you just stick in your suitcase," Liz finished the thought.

"You're right, she had to get a special vehicle just to transport it around Phoenix. Maybe we could rent one … "

"Out here in the boonies?" Liz snapped out of frustration. Seeing her mother's defensive expression, she quickly added, "sorry … " before Rachel could remind her that the "boonies" wasn't *her* idea.

"What about one of the relatives that plays the guitar? That would be nice."

"Mom, that was nice for you and Dad, two 60's hippies."

"We were not 60's hippies!"

"Were so!"

"Were what?" asked a chipper voice. Liz looked up to see Sean at the screen door, flushed and panting from his morning run.

"Nothing," said Liz. "Sean, Sophie cancelled! … She's had a death in the family … and can't be here, … which means the harp won't be here, either … Sean, what are we going to do?" Sean didn't seem to be getting it. Like many grooms-to-be, he was not as eager to be involved with the preparations as Liz would have liked.

"I don't know," he said, seemingly unconcerned. "But I'm sure you and your mom will come up with a solution," he added, patting her shoulder with a confident smile. "Well, I'd better get back and hop in the shower." And he left as carefree as he had arrived, while Liz's stress level went up another notch.

"Coward," she muttered under her breath.

Mother-of-the-bride was too busy thinking to hear her. She stared with knitted brow at the map of the area on the cover of the phone directory.

"OK," she began. "We're up here in northern Michigan [*which wasn't my idea*, Liz knew she was thinking] … on a beach. Piano, organ, out of the question … "

"A wedding without music!" Liz fretted. "I can just see me walking down the aisle in silence—or hey, maybe Dad could play his harmonica while we walk!" she added sarcastically.

"You don't have to get nasty about it … " Rachel muttered.

"I heard that!" Liz's father's voice yelled from the kitchen.

Suddenly Rachel blurted, "Interlochen!"

"Huh?"

"The Interlochen Academy for the Performing Arts is less than an hour away!"

"You think they have someone who'd help us out?"

"Well, we can try," Rachel said, picking up the phone and dialing.

"*Try?!* Mom, the wedding's in three days, we'll have to do more than try!"

"Yes, I'd like the number for the Interlochen Academy for the Performing Arts, please." Rachel had on her business voice. "Interlochen," she repeated. She paused, then scribbled down a phone number. "Thank you," she said and hung up. She immediately began dialing again.

After what seemed like an hour of silence, Rachel began, "Hello, I—" She stopped, sighed, and pressed "0" to bypass the rest of the menu.

No longer able to sit still, Liz decided to go down to the beach to try to walk off the stress. As she left, her mother's voice faded away.

"Hello … we have need of musicians …Yes, I'll hold."

The late summer waves pounded the shore, bringing back happy memories of endless August days of body surfing in the warmest water of the year. She remembered how she and her friends used to play in the waves for hours until their tired mothers, who had been watching and counting the bobbing heads, finally summoned them out for dinner.

Such a happy, carefree time it had been. And now in a few days Liz was to have what was traditionally the happiest day in a woman's life. She was about to marry the man she was in love with, and she looked forward more than anything to launching into a new life with him, with God's blessing, and watching His plans for them unfold. With all of these happy plans, why was she so stressed now? Why was she so impatient and irritated with everyone? Did it really matter if there wasn't a harpist for the wedding?

Well … *yes.*

Was it really that important that everything go *exactly* as planned? Did it have to be perfect?

Yes! It did! This wasn't just *a* wedding, this was *her* wedding. Hers and Sean's. Why go through a year of work and planning if it wasn't going to be the way they wanted it? Why battle with parents and explain to other traditionalists in order to have it their way only to have their way fall apart when the day came?

Why the myriad phone calls to find out most rental places in the area had very limited resources? Why try to reserve tables, chairs, and a tent from Grand Rapids, linens and dishes from Traverse City, flowers from Ludington, a photographer and cake from Manistee, and bring up rented tuxes from St. Louis? And then more phone calls each time they tried to confirm, only to hear, "I'm sorry, that doesn't seem to be in our system. What was your name again?" Liz really couldn't blame her mother for being stressed out and irritated. No wonder her parents hadn't seemed as thrilled with the uniqueness and creativity of their plans as she and Sean had been. Liz herself was beginning to wonder if the typical Ladue church-wedding-and-country-club-reception would have been such a bad idea after all.

Except now it was too late to go back and start over, even if she had wanted to. As it had occurred to her how far her mind and heart had strayed from the original idealistic plans, the tears started to spill over. *Three days to go, and what happened to the joy?* She wanted so much for her wedding to be a testimony to the goodness of God, especially to those relatives and acquaintances that would be there who had repeatedly turned down her invitations to go to church. She and Sean had carefully picked out the scriptures they wanted about Christ and the Church, His Bride. They had prayed that the presence of God would permeate the ceremony and everything that followed, and that He would be felt by everyone present.

But how was that going to happen with the bride being an irritable, perfectionist nervous wreck? She was tired—so tired—of running all day until exhausted, then fretting in the wee hours of the morning trying to get some sleep. She even resented Sean for not sharing the stress, for just basking in the joy of winning the love of his life. *The love of his life!* What an honor. Now she felt ungrateful and unworthy, too.

What's wrong with me? she prayed. She was marrying a man with all the godly qualities she could ever want in a husband, and all she felt was anger that he had "abandoned" her at the moment of crisis. Somewhere in the whirlwind of emotions a still, small voice spoke some reason to her and pointed out that she had done precisely the same thing to her mother, who was back at the cottage searching for musicians.

She found that she had been increasing the pace of her walk, and now she was a bit breathless, either from the brisk walk or from trying to hold back the sobs when an occasional walker would pass and say "good morning." She was relieved that she hadn't run into anyone she knew; she wasn't feeling particularly chatty. She turned around and jogged back to where Rachel sat by the phone, staring at the to-do list.

"Nice of you to come back," she commented, looking up momentarily. Liz didn't contest the indirect accusation.

"I'm sorry for deserting you like that," she apologized, pulling up a chair. "So what'd you find out?"

"The woman in the office said she'd put something on the bulletin board about our needing music Saturday," she said. "So I guess we'll just have to wait now."

Wait?! thought Liz. *This is torture!* She had a mental picture of a few people walking past the kiosk, scarcely glancing at the bulletin board, where a tiny Post-it said

"HELP!" She took a deep breath.

"So, what's next?" she asked, peering over at the desk. The calendar looked like an overused scratch pad. Appointments, parties, meetings, phones numbers, and addresses were crammed into every little box. A few business cards were stuck to the edges with paper clips. In spite of the wedding's being away from Ladue (which the kids facetiously called "Lah-dee-doo") in an out-of -the-way place, smaller, and presumably simpler, it seemed the complexities had definitely caught up with them. Locating the needed items and making sure they'd all be in the right place at the right time was only the beginning. Recording the RSVP's meant not only keeping track of the count, but also updating the number of reservations at the local motels.

Rachel fished through the clutter and came up with a list for the day's activities.

"Well," she said, "I'm still trying to get a hold of that florist to make sure the flowers are all set now. The last time I spoke to them, the man sounded either distracted or clueless. I had to go over the whole list all over again … I wonder if this is the florist that put gladiolas in the arrangements at Ashley Stuart's wedding … "

"Is that bad?" Liz wondered.

"Gladiolas are for funerals, dear," Rachel explained, as though this were something everyone should know. "Anyway," she said, getting back to the present situation, "I'd just feel better if we could have it confirmed—again."

"So would I," Liz agreed. Her mother dialed the number on the rotary phone that had been there for the past thirty years. Since the touch-tone answering machine next to it was only slightly newer and didn't always work, Rachel felt it was worth the extra seconds of dialing to be sure to get through. But to Liz the extra seconds seemed like half an hour.

"Hello," said Rachel, taking on her business voice again. "This is … " she stopped short and sighed. "Another menu," she scowled, hanging up and redialing on the touch tones.

"*Menu?* For *that* place? I've seen it, it's about the size of Aunt Ellen's living room," Liz scoffed.

"Well, dear, your Aunt Ellen does have a relatively large living room," said Rachel sarcastically. Liz rolled her eyes, and her mother smiled slightly. At least their mutual irritation was not at each other this time, and they began to feel a sense of camaraderie in fighting this battle together.

Liz heard a faint voice at the other end, saw her mother roll her eyes—very uncharacteristic of Rachel—and heard a distinctive "beep!"

"Hello, this is Rachel Danfield, calling about my daughter's upcoming wedding. I just wanted to make sure we were all set with the flowers. I had spoken to Dale, and I just wanted to confirm the list." She spoke slowly and distinctly, as though someone on the other end might be taking notes. It also sounded like someone telling a kindergartner how to set the table. "We have the bridal bouquet, three bridesmaids' bouquets, eight boutonnières, and three corsages. Also, there is a large bouquet for the altar and ten centerpieces with candles for the tables. Everything is red roses with ferns and baby's breath. I hope this matches your list. Please call and confirm that this matches your list and that it will all be delivered Saturday morning, September 8, to 9758 Lakeside Road. Our number here is ..."

As Rachel gave out the number, Liz sighed, thinking how all this calling was going to make them prisoners in the house for the rest of the day. Rachel must have read her mind, because she added,

"If you get our answering machine, please just leave us a message letting us know if things are all set. Thank you." She hung up the phone and sighed heavily. "OK, that's one thing we can cross off the list ... " She appeared to have second thoughts. "Or maybe we shouldn't cross it off until we hear from them ... "

"OK, so can we please get out of the house now?" Liz pleaded. All the stress seemed to make the walls close in, and there was plenty to do in town as well.

"Well, I'm sorry, Elizabeth, but I'm still trying to contact that caterer, and we really need to confirm the tent rental in case it rains ... "

Please don't let it rain! Liz pleaded silently.

"You know, dear, you still have a table full of lovely gifts from the shower last week. Why don't you write some thank-you notes while I finish up here?"

"OK," Liz agreed. How could she complain with so much loot piled up in her honor?

Just then George, father-of-the-bride, appeared in the doorway wearing a turquoise golf shirt and colorful plaid shorts. He had a half-eaten sweet roll in one hand and a cup of coffee in the other.

"Looks like a lot of activity in here. Anything I can do to help?" he asked innocently. He sounded so childlike and carefree Liz didn't know whether to kiss him or shake him into reality. The question was moot anyway, since he was due at the golf course in fifteen minutes.

"Yes, dear, you can help by getting out from under foot." Rachel knew how to get to the point with her husband.

"You got it!" George replied cheerfully. Liz smiled, knowing this was not the first time he had received this direction from his wife. He took one last bite of the sweet roll, finished the coffee, and set the cup and napkin on the already overcrowded table. Ignoring Rachel's look of irritation, he grabbed his golf clubs from the closet and headed for the door. "Have a wonderful day."

"You, too. Have a good game," said Rachel absently as she dialed the next number.

"'bye, Dad. Have fun." As the sound of George's happy whistling faded, Liz searched the desk for a pen that worked. One by one she scratched the pad of paper, and with each unsuccessful attempt her irritation increased.

"Why do we keep all these pens around that don't work?!" she fumed, throwing the nonfunctioning ones back into the drawer.

"Yes, I'm calling about the tent for the Danfield/O'Brien wedding Saturday ... " Rachel began politely. " ... Yes, I'll hold ... " she sighed. Liz turned back to the table of gifts.

The summer people had generously thrown a couple's shower for Liz and Sean, so along with the kitchen and bath supplies, Sean was presented with an impressive array of tools, a grill, and other "guy stuff." When Liz had told him privately that it "would be nice" if he'd do some of the thank-you notes, he seemed agreeable enough. Whether or not he was ever going to follow through remained to be seen. The gifts were neatly arranged on and around the card table in the living room, with the "guy stuff" in a separate pile. The other gifts gave Liz emotions ranging from gratitude to apprehension. All those household items—would she do a good job with them? Did Sean really like her cooking, or did he just like *her*? She had never managed a household before, and the thought made her feel a little overwhelmed. Then she'd smile, remembering what a sweet, patient man she was marrying. Even if he wouldn't write thank-you notes.

She had just begun the first thank-you note when she heard the ringtone of her cell phone. Pleasantly surprised that she was getting a signal today, she stepped out onto the deck that overlooked Lake Michigan. The Danfields had had the cottage built into the side of the dune for this very scenic view, and today it was glorious. Liz settled into one of the loungers before answering.

"Hello?—Elaine!" she cried. Something about hearing her sister's voice made her feel less alone in her struggles, probably because she and her sister always managed to be allies, as different as they were. Sure, they had fought like rabid pit bulls as kids, but when they had reached high school and opposition from the outside—judgmental "cool" people, "mean" teachers, and heart-breaking boys—Elaine had taken on the role of protector for her little sister. Now that they rarely saw each other, they had become the best of friends.

"Hey sis! How's the bride doing?"

"Going crazy! Everyone around here acts like this is the first time there was ever a wedding."

"One like you've got cooked up, it is. Gee, so you think it's too late to just do it at church and have the reception at the country club?"

"Don't *you* start with me now!" Liz threatened. Elaine laughed out loud.

"Are they giving you guys a hard time about your 'unique' plans?" she asked.

"If by 'they' you mean Mom, the caterer, the florist, the rental people, the bridal shop, the ... yes," she sighed.

"Don't worry, little sis, I'll be there tomorrow, and you won't be so outnumbered. What's Sean doing?"

"He's at the cottage his folks rented, taking a leisurely shower. I don't know what his plans are for today, but I have a feeling they don't include helping me."

"Men."

"So how's Rick?" Liz asked out of habit, but she had second thoughts the moment she asked. Elaine's boyfriend had been a subject that caused considerable friction with her parents. Although he and Elaine had moved in together, George and Rachel refused to treat him like a member of the family, since technically he wasn't. Liz and Sean had been conflicted over the issue, for although they didn't agree with Elaine and Rick's choice of lifestyle, they didn't want to be unloving toward two people who needed the Lord as much as anybody did. They finally had decided to invite Rick to the wedding. George and Rachel had agreed reluctantly but made it clear that while Elaine was welcome to stay in the family summer home, Rick would have to find other accommodations. Elaine had taken this as the ultimate insult, but Rick had quietly backed off, saying he had plans of his own that weekend anyway. So Elaine was coming alone.

"Rick's fine," she said. "He's getting together with his little nephews this weekend. They adore him."

"So what time's your flight get in again?" Liz asked, anxious to change the subject.

"6:30."

"Can't wait to see you! Hey, let's get Dad to take us to dinner at that resort on the bay."

"Sounds great. I'm guessing Mom could use the break."

"*Mom* needs a break?! She's not the only one."

"Well, you know how Dad likes to spend money on everybody. This would be a pretty good time for him to indulge us all."

"Yeah," Liz laughed. "So far all he's done is 'stay out from under foot.'" Elaine laughed knowingly.

"Well, that and footing the bill for the whole wedding."

"True, I should keep that in mind." Talking to Elaine always lightened the mood.

"Is Mom busy?" asked Elaine. (Silence.) "I mean, can she talk?"

Liz opened the sliding door a crack to hear, "No, *this* Saturday … September 8 … We *didn't* change the date, it's *always* been this Saturday … "

"I think maybe you'd better talk to her later, she's kind of in the middle of something right now."

"OK, well, maybe you guys can get back to me later. Call me on my cell, OK?"

"OK, I'll add that to our list. Love ya!"

"Love ya back!"

Liz hung up about the same time as Rachel did, and stepping inside, she was alarmed to see her mother with her head in her hands.

"What's wrong, Mom?!" she cried.

"They didn't have us in their 'system,' so either their computer messed up or someone deleted us." Rachel had always referred to herself as "technologically challenged." She joked about having to be dragged kicking and screaming into the twenty-first century. All this trouble with computers was not convincing her to stop resisting.

"So are we without a tent?" Liz gasped.

"No, according to the man I talked to, we have one now, but it isn't the one we originally wanted, and he sounded pretty put out about it."

"*He* was put out?" It was only 10:00 in the morning, and Rachel seemed exhausted already. Suddenly Liz began to feel sorry for someone besides herself. It wasn't fair that her mom had been putting in all this time and effort only to have incompetent people mad at her. Impulsively, Liz leaned over and gave her a hug.

"Thanks, Mom," she said. "Come on, let's go check on the dresses, and then I'll buy you lunch."

"OK, I'll check on the dresses, but you don't need to buy me lunch."

"Oh yes, I do."

"No you don't."

"Yes I do."

"No you don't … "

CHAPTER THREE

The trip into town ended up taking virtually all day. The alterations on Rachel's dress weren't quite right, and though the tailor promised to have it perfect by Saturday, it gave Rachel one more piece of unfinished business to stress over. The tailor, reluctant to admit to being at fault, asked the mother of the bride if she had put on a few pound since the last fitting. This did not help Rachel's mood one bit, and she ordered the "lite plate" for lunch.

They stopped in at the bakery to make sure everything was on schedule with the wedding cake, but the woman who was in charge of their order was home with a sick child, and the young girl she had left to watch the shop knew even less about computers than Rachel did and didn't know how to check on it.

Such non-accomplishments went on until about 4:30, when the two headed back to the cottage, exhausted and one day closer to the wedding.

"I wish I could check off just one thing on this list!" Rachel fretted. Liz tried to think of something encouraging to say, but at the moment she was as frustrated as her mother and was afraid that if she opened her mouth she would burst into tears.

It was 4:55 when they stepped into the cottage. Liz saw a red light blinking from across the room.

"We got a message, Mom!" she cried, running over to the answering machine. She pressed the button to listen.

"Hello, Mrs. Danfield," came the chipper voice. "This is Larry at the Fresh-as-a-Daisy Floral Shop. I got your message …"

"Thank goodness!" said Rachel.

"I was just returning your call."

"And the flowers … ???"

"Have a nice day." The machine clicked off.

"So, are we set for flowers or not?" Liz wondered.

"I don't know!" snapped Rachel, who, having another basis for saying I-told-you-so, was not getting much satisfaction from it. "All this cutting-edge, high-tech equipment, and people still don't know how to communicate!" For a moment Liz was afraid her mother was going to smash the machine. And if the machine was going to get smashed, she at least wanted the satisfaction of doing it herself.

"Well, let's call him again," Liz sighed. "Did he leave his number?"

"No, of course not," Rachel griped, sorting through her Post-its and finally thumbing through the phone book. "… Here it is … 723 … " As she dictated, Liz dialed and set the phone on "Speaker" so she could listen in.

"Hello, you've reached Fresh-as-a-Daisy Floral Shop. We are presently closed. Please call us during normal business hours. Goodbye." >click<

"And what, pray tell, are normal business hours?!" Liz demanded, holding the receiver in a stranglehold and looking at the clock, which registered 5:01.

"Not after 5:00, apparently," said Rachel, sinking into the big armchair. "I'm whipped, Elizabeth. I'm sorry, I just can't do this." Liz had never before seen her mother so close to bawling.

They were both startled to hear a sweet voice coming from the kitchen.

"Maybe it's time to call in reinforcements." A tiny elderly lady appeared in the doorway.

"Nana! You're here!" Liz cried. "We didn't see your car … ?"

"Bapa noticed you were out of snacks, so he went to 'the village' to get some."

Something about hearing her grandmother's voice calling her grandfather 'Bapa,' talking about snacks, and referring to 'the village' stirred up in Liz such happy memories that a brief wave of childhood-summer-vacation peace came over her. It made her remember why she had wanted to get married here in the first place.

She ran to hug her grandmother, and the frail little arms somehow managed to give her enough strength to go on. Rachel must have felt the same, because she got up from the big chair and sank into the motherly embrace, where she lingered for a moment longer than usual.

"Mother, I'm so glad you're here." Rachel's voice was muffled in Nana's shoulder. Nana just held her, smiled serenely, and gave Liz a wink.

Two hours later both the bride's and groom's families were crowded around the dining room table, enjoying Nana's delicious home-cooked stew and sharing the events (or non-events) of the day. Liz learned that her husband-to-be had not been goofing off all day as she had accused him of doing, but had been helping his parents with plans for the rehearsal dinner. She realized that this project must be as challenging as theirs, since they were in a rented cottage in a place that was still relatively new to them. Liz wondered if they had met with as much frustration as she and her mother had. The stories they told would indicate "yes," but they seemed none the worse for the experience.

"Isn't it interestin'," said Sean's mother Colleen, "that even in a quaint little town like this, it's still so hard to talk to a livin', breathin' person?" As different as these women were, suddenly there was a connection that was bigger than Rachel's upper-class breeding or Colleen's life struggles in her native Ireland.

"Yes! Amazing, isn't it?" Rachel agreed. "We still haven't got the flowers confirmed. All I can reach are voice mails and menus!"

Sean's brother Michael laughed. "If you're having a wedding, press '1.' If you're having a funeral, press '2.' If you've forgotten your wife's birthday—"

"—press '2,'" George guessed. Rachel tried to give him a dirty look but couldn't keep a straight face. Sean's father, "Pastor Dan," joined in.

"If you forgot her birthday, and it's today, hang up and dial '911.'"

"Ye'd better believe it!" added Colleen, whose Irish dialect came out mainly when she was scolding, warning, or giving orders. (Or in this case, all three.)

"If you want daisies, press '4.' If you want chrysanthemums, press '5,'" giggled Sean's teenaged sister Shannon.

"If you want gladiolas for a wedding, hang up, you don't know what you're doing!" Rachel finished the menu with a hearty laugh. Everyone joined in the laughter, but as the men glanced at each other, clueless, the women laughed all the more; Rachel laughed until the tears came.

Liz could feel the tension leave as she relaxed and enjoyed the moment. She was grateful to see Rachel savoring the meal she hadn't had to cook and joking about the things that had had her close to tears earlier. From the moment the families had joined hands and Pastor Dan had prayed over the meal and the two families about to be joined together, something had changed. It had been as if God had been waiting all day for someone to invite Him to participate in what was happening, and the moment He was asked, He had made His presence known with the sense that everything was going to be fine and they should just enjoy the ride. If He could part the Red Sea and raise the dead, He could probably work out the details of a wedding.

"I found a little fabric shop in Manistee today," said Shannon. "I got some white tulle and ribbon for the birdseed."

"Birdseed?" Bapa asked.

"Honey, people don't throw rice at weddings anymore," Nana explained. "They throw birdseed. Don't you remember the Donnelsons' daughter's wedding?"

"Oh yeah," he recalled. "I just thought they did that because the groom was a bit of a flake."

"Lewis!" Nana scolded.

"Dad, they found out that rice can hurt the birds if they eat it," Rachel explained.

"Yeah, Bapa. They eat it, then when they drink water it makes the rice swell up in their stomachs."

"And they explode?" her grandfather guessed.

"If you ask me, that'd be a lot more interesting to watch than the wedding!" said Michael.

"Behave yersilf, Michael!" said his mother.

"Well, we have plenty of birdseed," said Rachel. "Every year when we come up in May, George forgets we already have half a ton, and he buys enough for two summers."

"I'm just stocking up so we don't have to buy any later," George explained defensively.

"Then later he forgets again and buys more."

"Thanks for getting that stuff, Shannon," said Liz. "After Elaine and my friend Sarah get here we can have some 'girl time' and make the bundles."

Later when the O'Brien's had gone back to their rental, Bapa, Rachel, and George retired for the night. Liz was ready for bed but seeing some lights on in the living room, she came out to turn them off. She was surprised to hear Nana still in the kitchen, cleaning up. She didn't seem the least bit tired but hummed an old tune Liz recognized but couldn't quite identify.

"Nana! I'm sorry you got left to clean up all this. Can I help you?"

"Liz, sweetie! You're still up?—Oh, I'm just about finished … Well, here, you want to put this away?" She handed Liz the casserole she had just dried, and Liz put it in the cupboard as Nana dried the salad bowl.

"That was a wonderful dinner, Nana. How did you pull it off in so little time?"

"Oh, I just fixed everything at home this morning and put it in a cooler. All I had to do when we got here was heat it up."

"Well, it was delicious. Thank you so much!"

"Well, I had a feeling your mother would be under some stress, and she didn't need the extra burden of feeding everyone."

"Yeah, we had pretty much decided on a restaurant, but that would have been noisy … and expensive." She smiled at the mental picture of the way her father always faked a heart attack when he got the bill. "This was so much nicer. Everyone was able to get acquainted."

"Your Sean has such a nice family, dear."

"He does. And I know they love you already."

"Well, you know the way to a man's heart … "

"… is through his stomach," Liz finished the proverb.

"And the way to a woman's heart is telling her she doesn't have to cook tonight," added Nana with a wink. "Now you must be exhausted after such a big day. You'd better get some sleep."

"I don't know if I can sleep, Nana. Only two more days to prepare, and there are still so many problems!" Liz was horrified to feel the stress start to come back after the evening reprieve. Nana put her arm around her granddaughter.

"Now you know it's all going to come together, and it'll be beautiful," she reassured her. "I can already sense the Lord's blessing on this marriage. Besides, all the 'problems' and unexpected things are what make it memorable. These are things you'll be telling your grandchildren someday and laughing about."

"I'm not laughing now," Liz sighed.

"No, right now everything seems so serious—and a wedding is serious, but it's always an occasion with flawed people, so it helps to keep a sense of humor." She smiled as though enjoying a private joke. "You know, Liz, when Bapa and I got married, he was very nervous, but he was determined not to let anyone know. He was going to be the pillar of strength, my knight in shining armor! When the minister asked, 'Wilt thou take this woman—' he blurted out 'I wilt!'—then passed out cold. I was mortified! Thought my world had come to an end, and this was the worst day of my life.

"But when he came to a few minutes later, the first thing he did was look into my eyes and ask, 'Are we married yet?' We finished the ceremony as if nothing had happened. Afterward he looked at me and said, 'Honey, do you feel OK? You don't look so well.' I began to see the humor in it, and we've been laughing about it ever since. I can't tell you how many times he's told that story, and every time he does, it gets a laugh, and no one laughs harder than he does."

Liz was laughing herself

"Thanks, Nana. I need to be reminded of that. I just can't help wanting everything to be perfect. I mean, this isn't just a wedding, it's *my* wedding."

Nana chuckled. "You and your mother have always been such perfectionists. This is northern Michigan, honey. Look around you. The woods, the lake, the dunes—perfection is everywhere."

"Yeah, but the people are another story!" Liz complained.

"Yes, we are, aren't we?" Nana laughed. The two hugged. Then Nana took Liz's face in her hands and looked into her eyes. "Now you just remember, Elizabeth Danfield-soon-to-be-O'Brien, if God takes care of the little birds—who blow up if they eat rice—He's going to be able to take care of you two little lovebirds."

" … 'His Eye Is on the Sparrow.' Is that what you were humming in the kitchen just now?"

"Probably. I guess it's one of my favorites. Now, I know you've had a lot on your mind today, but now it's time to turn it off and go to sleep."

She makes it sound so easy, Liz thought.

"Show me where the switch is, and I'll turn it off," she grumbled.

"Just give it to Jesus, honey. He's going to be up all night anyway. You know He wants it to be beautiful, too, and He'll be glorified when it is."

"Thanks, Nana. And thanks again for dinner."

"My pleasure, dear."

Liz began to leave, then stopped in the doorway and turned to her grandmother.

"Nana, do you know what my earliest memory is?"

"What's that, sweetie?"

"You kneeling by my crib and praying over me. I remember wondering what you were doing. Now I know how important it was."

Nana smiled. "It still is. And I still do."

CHAPTER FOUR

September 6, 2001

Liz was awakened by the sound of the phone, and Rachel's chipper, polite voice told her that her mother was already up. She opened her bedroom door a crack to hear half the conversation.

"Oh—Yes! Thank you so much for calling. Our harpist had a death in the family and cancelled ... and you're a harpist? ... oh ... oh, how lovely. And you're available Saturday?...Yes, day after tomorrow (oh my!)...Wonderful! I'll speak to my daughter, but I'm sure it'll be fine ... Well, yes, I suppose we could do that. ... Yes, now that you mention it, that would be a good idea ... "

As Rachel was getting the necessary information, Liz thanked the Lord for answering her (and Nana's) prayers. She had a harpist!

"So what's going on?" she asked eagerly when her mother had hung up. "We have a harpist?"

"Um, no," said Rachel, and Liz's heart sank again. "We have a woodwind quartet."

"A woodwind ... ?"

"I know it's not what you had in mind, but when you think about it, it might sound nice."

I don't want nice, I want beautiful! "I'm .. trying to imagine it ... "

"Well, instead of imagining it, we could drive up to Interlochen, meet them, and hear them play. They said they'd be happy to audition for us."

Liz laughed at the thought of the word that used to strike fear into her heart, realizing she was on the other end of it now.

"Well, we don't exactly have a huge selection to choose from, but I would feel better if I could hear them."

"Well, Elaine's plane gets into Traverse City tonight, so I told them we could meet them about 5:00."

"5:00?!" Liz cried. "Do we have to wait that long? Couldn't we go up this morning?" She was beginning to feel the stress close in on her again. It crossed her mind that she was starting to sound like a spoiled brat, but her mother understood completely.

"I was hoping you'd say that," said Rachel, grinning and grabbing the phone. "Music is such a big part of the wedding, I think we should go as soon as possible, for our own peace of mind. I'll call them right back."

"Thank you, Mom!" Liz hugged her mother. "I'll get dressed."

She dressed in record time and called Sean to see if he wanted to come. She was a bit miffed at him for telling her to go on without him, and that he was going to play tennis with Michael. But he said he trusted her judgment, so she accepted that this was going to be another day of "girl time." When she hung up, she turned to see her mother and grandmother waiting for her.

"Nana! Are you coming, too?"

"If you don't mind, dear. I'd love to hear this quartet, too."

"I don't mind at all. It'll be fun! What's that, Nana?" she asked, pointing to the faded, worn book her grandmother was holding.

"It's an old hymnal I found in the piano bench. I thought I'd bring it, in case you wanted them to play something from it."

Liz didn't have the heart to tell her that she and Sean were planning to have contemporary worship songs played, not some dusty old hymns, although at the time she had a hard time hearing a woodwind quartet playing either. She was starting to get a knot in her stomach as she began to feel she was losing control of her own wedding that she had planned so meticulously. She didn't mind input, but she felt there was beginning to be a few too many opinions.

"Thank you for meeting with us on such short notice. You are just wonderful to do this!"

As Rachel gushed, Liz began sizing up the players. Three out of the four seemed to her to be extremely young to be professional musicians, but then she realized these must be students, probably teenagers. One had about three days' worth of thin beard growth and hair that her grandmother was probably thinking looked a bit "scruffy."

One was a young girl wearing no makeup who had a long red braid down her back. The third wore thick glasses and appeared to be about twelve years old, and the one adult of the group was in his fifties and had silver streaks in his thinning hair.

These are the people who are going to save the day? she thought skeptically.

When Rachel was finished with the preliminary small talk, the musicians took out their instruments and sat down at their music stands.

"What were you thinking you'd like played?" asked the older one, who appeared to be the teacher. "We have Mozart, Schubert, Schumann … "

"Well," said Liz, "we were wondering if you had anything a bit more … contemporary. Do you know 'Breathe'?" The musicians exchanged blank glances. " 'Shout to the Lord'?" Again, no sign of recognition.

"Do you have the sheet music for those pieces?" the girl asked, trying to be helpful.

"No, the guys at the church just kinda play the chords by ear and sing."

Great! she thought. *Classical music is nice and all, but it isn't me and Sean.*

"How about some hymns?" Nana's sweet voice piped up.

Old hymns now? This can't be happening! And the knot tightened.

Nana handed the hymnal to the teacher.

"Sure," he said. "They're usually easy to play." He smiled as he looked through the first few pages. "Yep. They're all arranged in four parts. The flute does the soprano and so on. No problem."

No problem for you maybe …

"Are these the ones you want to hear?" the teacher asked, and Liz noticed little slips of paper placed between the pages. Nana had been finding her favorites and marking them in the car on the way up.

Her favorites!? But it's our wedding!

"Just some ideas," said Nana. "Liz will be the one deciding." Liz could feel Nana's hand stroking her back comfortingly. "How about starting with number 114?"

"OK." The teacher flipped to the spot and put the book on the stand. They all four picked up their instruments and gathered around. The three students squinted slightly, and it was obvious by the looks on their faces that they had never played this particular hymn before.

Oh well, they have two days to practice.

The students were poised and waiting for the teacher's signal. At his nod, they began.

Within seconds Liz was reminded that this was Interlochen Academy for the Performing Arts, not just a music school, but the one that attracted the best of the best. The most gifted young people in the country—or for that matter, from all over the world—came there to prepare for a lifetime of performing. Even the prepubescent musician, who was barely bigger than his instrument, played flawlessly, and the four were so in tune with one another that it was almost like listening to one instrument— one incredibly beautiful instrument. Liz felt as though the sky had opened, and celestial birds were singing in a heavenly language. It sounded so different, yet she recognized the song this time: "His Eye Is on the Sparrow."

Her eyes filled with tears, not stressful tears this time but tears of awe. This was truly an answer to prayer. It was exactly what she had wanted; she just hadn't known it until that moment. She laid her head on Nana's shoulder, as Rachel took her hand, and the three of them drank in the wonder of the moment.

When the song was finished, the musicians looked up. "Was that all right?" the teacher asked. Liz almost laughed at the absurdity of the question. She tried to answer but found that she couldn't speak.

"It was lovely," said Rachel, and Liz noticed she had a rare look of serenity on her face. She took the hymnal and paged through some of the parts Nana had marked. "How about this one?" she asked.

As they began to play "This Is My Father's World," she whispered to Liz, "We used to sing this one at camp years ago. It's so fitting out here with all this natural beauty." Liz noticed a catch in her mother's voice.

As each song played, the stress was replaced with a peaceful delight. Liz and Sean had prayed that their wedding would glorify Christ, so it wasn't a matter of what the two of them wanted. It wasn't about them, it was about *Him*. Liz began to realize that many of these "dusty old hymns" had been resurrected and played on Christian radio in contemporary styles, complete with electric guitars, drums, and synthesizers. Their friends would recognize the songs they'd grown to love. At the same time, the older generations would recognize songs they had heard in churches all their lives, but with pianos and organs. Now, with this quartet, every song was fresh and new again.

"Well, what do you think, honey?" Rachel asked, and this time Liz was able to get out a couple of words as she stated the obvious.

"It's perfect."

CHAPTER FIVE

The three women were in high spirits as they took the scenic drive back to the cottage, stopping at a lookout point to admire the view. Liz, thinking she had not done enough working out (just stressing out) lately, climbed the 150 steps to the very top to take in the early autumn sunshine and feel the fresh breeze blowing her hair.

Her hair!

Her momentary reprieve from the pre-wedding tension came to an abrupt stop, and she fairly bounded back down the dune.

"Mom," she asked breathlessly. "Did you ever make that appointment for me to get my hair done Saturday?"

"Did *I* do it?" said Rachel. "I thought you told me *you* were doing it!"

"No, I told you I wanted Yolanda to do my hair." That pesky knot was back.

"I didn't know that meant *I* was supposed to do it," Rachel began, but she just finished with "We'd better call her right away!" She reached into the car for the extra phone book she had put there for just such an emergency.

Good ol' think-ahead Mom! Liz thought in spite of her annoyance with the misunderstanding. Rachel gave her the number, and Liz dialed it on her cell phone but got no response. She looked at the screen: no bars.

"Oh, great! We aren't getting any reception out here!" she cried.

"Something wrong?" asked Nana, coming back from the lookout deck.

"I hope not," said Rachel, "but we need to get back *now*."

They jumped into the car and headed back for "the village" to talk to Yolanda.

"Phew!" thought Liz as they stepped into the salon and were greeted with enough fumes to fill a stadium. *I could never work in a place like this all day!*

"Hi, can I help y—oh, Mrs. Danfield! Hello! Hi Liz!" A middle-aged woman greeted them. "I hear congratulations are in order!"

"Yes, actually that's why we're here," said Rachel. It was not like her to cut through the small talk, but as she explained the situation, Liz was horrified to see the beautician's face turn from smiles to concern, to sympathy.

"Oh honey," she said to Liz. "I'm so sorry, I'm completely booked Saturday. There's another wedding in town, and my girls and I are doing the hair for the bride and all the bridesmaids. You might try one of the shops in Manistee … "

But they were to discover that after a long summer of catering to the resort crowd, most beauticians were taking some well-deserved vacations the week after Labor Day. They returned to the cottage having made no appointments.

"Honey, your hair is beautiful just the way it is," said Nana, stroking Liz's long curls. "It looked like this when you met Sean, and it looked like this when he fell in love with you, so maybe you should just … "

"But I wanted something extra special on my special day!" Liz insisted. "Two years ago when I saw what Yolanda did with Amy Peterson's hair, I decided that was exactly the way I wanted it when I got married."

"But now that style's two years old," Rachel pointed out, trying her best to sound snooty and make Liz lighten up. It didn't help, so she decided this might be a good time to change the subject. "Let's check on those roses, shall we?"

"Roses?" said Nana. "How lovely!"

"It's 'our' flower," Liz explained. "When Sean and I were at U. of I., he sent me a red rose on opening night—anonymously."

"How romantic!" Nana exclaimed, and the way she was settling into the armchair, looking at Liz expectantly, it was clear she wanted to hear the whole story.

"It sat in my dressing room in a Coke bottle the entire show, with me wondering who it was from—and trying to concentrate on putting on my makeup." Nana gave her a mischievous grin. "Actually, I thought it was from this other guy that I knew liked me." And Liz told her the whole story about Aaron, the understudy that had kissed her on stage, and then off stage and had seemed very serious about her. The feeling had been mutual, and all seemed well until Liz's friend Sarah, a Christian, had counseled her about being "unequally yoked with an unbeliever." Sarah had convinced Liz that she was flirting with disaster, and when it was apparent that Aaron didn't plan on converting any time soon, Liz had ended it, but not without some agonizing.

"Well, thank the Lord for Sarah!" Nana declared. "If it weren't for her, you could have been planning a wedding with an unbeliever—and starting a life of heartache!"

"Yes, I can't imagine spending the rest of my life with anyone but Sean," Liz admitted. "Hey Nana! You'll get to meet Sarah tomorrow night. She's my other bridesmaid."

"I can't wait!" Nana exclaimed, taking Liz's hands as they shared a moment of excitement. Then they noticed Rachel looked frustrated again as she hung up the phone and turned to them.

"What's wrong, Mom?" Liz asked apprehensively.

"Oh, I still can't reach that silly florist! He's still 'away from his desk'!" Nana stifled a smirk at hearing Rachel call the man "silly," but Liz's smile faded.

"You mean we're *still* not 100% sure on the roses?" she cried.

"Well, his message yesterday sounded pretty upbeat, but maybe we'd better just go there, just in case. It's only 4:10, and it takes us about half an hour to get into town, so we should easily get there before five."

"Well, let's go!" said Nana, heading for the door, and Liz hoped that when she was that age she would have half the energy her grandmother had.

"CLOSED?!" Rachel shrieked as they pulled up and saw the sign in the window. "Liz, go see if anyone's still there." Liz jumped out and ran to the door. She sighed heavily and returned to the car.

"There's no one there, and they closed at 4:30," she said and promptly burst into tears.

"There's a message!" said Rachel as they entered the cottage. Liz ran to press the button, and the same cheery voice they had heard before said,

"This is Larry again from Fresh-as-a-Daisy. It's about 4:15, and I'm returning your call. I guess you're it." Liz rolled her eyes. "—oh by the way, just a reminder—we close at 4:30." ("Yes, we know that," muttered Rachel.) "Have a nice day!" And as the machine clicked off, Liz kicked the table savagely.

"Give us a hint, you son-of-a—silly person!" she stammered, seeing the shocked looks on the faces of the other two. There was a moment of silence, after which Nana broke into a fit of uncontrollable laughter. Rachel did not see the humor in the situation. Listening to her mother's giggles for about half a minute only increased her irritation.

"Mother, you sound drunk," she grumbled. This apparently only increased Nana's amusement, but she finally managed to contain herself.

"I'm sorry, honey," she said, catching her breath. But Liz could tell she was not as concerned as they were. Maybe she didn't care as much, but it seemed more likely she knew something they didn't.

"Well, I guess there's tomorrow," Rachel sighed.

Elaine was flying in that night, but after being in the car most of the day Liz didn't really want to climb back in and go another two hours. She was wondering how she could express this without hurting anyone's feelings when, as if reading her mind, Nana suggested that the "older folks" go fetch the bridesmaid and let the bride and groom have some time together to unwind. Liz quietly agreed, although she felt like throwing her arms around her grandmother in gratitude.

"Well," said Nana to the others, winking, "You know how those sisters are once they get together. They'll be talking nonstop until the wedding. So this'll be our one chance to get a word in edgewise with Elaine."

So that evening after a light supper of leftover stew, Liz and Sean took a long walk on the beach, and she told him of all her frustrations of the day. He listened patiently and tried to reassure her that everything would be fine in the end.

"After all," he said, "the important thing is that God brought us together, and if that's the case, who cares if we have a million roses?" (*Spoken like a true male*, Liz thought, sighing.)

"I don't think you get it," she said through clenched teeth. "This is our wedding day, the day we'll always remember, the one we'll have pictures of, in an album, an heirloom we'll show our children and grandchildren—through the generations they'll be able to see what our wedding looked like." She was starting to cry. "And it was supposes to have roses—the red roses that are the symbol of our love and ... and joy! ... And what are you smirking about?!"

"Nothing!" said Sean hastily. "OK, OK, our love and joy ... geez, don't yell at me!"

He didn't mean for her to hear him mutter "they're only flowers" under his breath, but she did.

"And I suppose this is only my hair!" The thought of her dashed dreams for the fairy-tale princess hair brought on another wave of self-pity. "I wanted that wonderful up-do for my hair, too, and it was going to be so perfect!" she sobbed. The wind was whipping her hair around, and she angrily tried to brush it out of her face. Sean turned her toward the wind and held her face in both hands, gazing at her.

"I don't know if this is the best time to tell you this," he began, hesitantly, "but it might help."

"What?" she sniffed, trying to get a grip.

"I love your hair. I love it down, and I love it just held back loosely in two clips the way you sometimes do. To be perfectly honest, if you'd gone out and gotten it done up like a clipper ship, I would've been pretty ticked." There was a brief silence during which Liz let the statement sink in and determined that he was sincere.

"Really?"

"Really. I never could understand why girls would do that complicated thing to their hair for proms and weddings and stuff. It's like the female equivalent of a tuxedo—which most of us guys also can't stand, by the way."

Well, now I know why guys don't enjoy formal things.

"So … the fact that my hair will be the same-ol'-same-ol' … "

" … is fine with me. If I'd known you were planning to do anything else, I would've said something sooner and saved you some aggravation. Anyway, I'm really glad you aren't wasting your parents' money making yourself … well, making yourself not look like *you*."

Liz breathed a sigh of relief. "Wow, I am, too. And now I don't have to inhale salon fumes for three hours, either."

"Yeah. Now see how things work out?" Sean said with his endearing wink and thumbs-up.

They had reached the largest dune of the area, one some people called "Apron Bluff," presumably because at one time it resembled an apron. Some called it "Old Baldy," but Liz's cousins had always called it "Merry Mountain." She had no idea why. They looked up at the sandy giant towering over them.

"Wanna climb it?" said Sean.

Liz accepted the challenge, and about thirty minutes later they stood at the top, panting.

"Wow, that's a bigger climb than I expected!" Sean gasped. Liz was too out of breath to answer. "If you climbed this every day, you'd really be in shape!" Liz shot him a dirty look. "—I don't mean 'you' personally, I mean anybody that climbed … I mean, you're in great shape! I love your shape!—I mean—"

"Give up, hon," Liz laughed. "Just enjoy the view."

They were so high up they could actually see the slight curve of the earth on the horizon. The sun, a giant red ball, hovered just over the water.

"Y'know, Liz, with all the hassles, I think it'll still be worth it to have the wedding here."

"Easy for you to say, Mr. Gotta-go-play-tennis-now," she teased. "But you're probably right. A Lah-dee-doo wedding in the church with a country club reception—now *that* would be same-ol'-same-ol'."

CHAPTER SIX

September 7, 2001

Friday morning was buzzing with activity. Elaine was the first one up in spite of the time change and the fact that she had missed her connection and hadn't arrived until after midnight. While she was out on the beach doing her yoga, Rachel was making a shopping list for her trip to "the village." Although Colleen and Shannon were in charge of the rehearsal dinner, somehow Sean's family had found out about the watermelon swans Rachel could carve, and with very little arm-twisting they had persuaded her to prepare a fruit salad for the occasion.

George sat at the breakfast table sipping his coffee as though nothing unusual were happening that day. He finished reading one section of the paper and dropped it on the floor as he started the next section. Rachel looked up from her list, her eyebrows furrowed. Contritely, George picked it back up and set it by his plate.

"Anything I can do to get out from under foot today?" he asked with childlike helpfulness. Rachel thought a moment and her face brightened.

"Come to think of it, there is," she said, opening the phone book and jotting down an address. Would you go to Manistee and check on the flowers for tomorrow? I don't have time to be calling that silly man all day."

"What do you want me to tell him?"

Rachel searched the desk until she found the piece of paper she was looking for.

"Here, take this," she said, handing him the paper. "This is the list of everything we need. He should have it all set, but the way things have been going … just make sure he has it scheduled for delivery *tomorrow!*"

"Leave the silly man to me!" George declared with an enthusiastic salute. He pulled his keys from his pocket, took two steps toward the door, came back to the table, grabbed the remainder of his English muffin, and was gone. As if on cue, Nana emerged from the kitchen and cleared his dishes. Rachel smiled at her; things seemed to be going like clockwork.

But the day was still young.

"Hit the floor runnin', huh Mom?"

Rachel looked up from the table to see Liz in the doorway with a sleepy smile on her face.

"'Tis ever thus," she sighed dramatically. "I just talked to the motel, and they're ready for the stampede," she added.

"Cool. And when's the 'stampede' due to arrive?"

"Oh, they'll be flocking in all day. We probably won't see most of them until the dinner tonight—at least, I hope we don't. We have a lot to do, and I don't really have time to entertain."

"Oh, they understand that, Mom."

"Sis!" called a voice from the deck. The sliding glass door opened, and the two auburn-haired girls squealed with delight and did their "sisterly dance" that had been their traditional greeting since the year they had first experienced separation and learned how much they actually missed each other. Nana giggled; Rachel shook her head and smiled.

"So what's on the 'genda today?" Elaine asked her mother.

"You really want to know?" said Rachel, holding up the list.

"Hey, we're on it, Mom! Just tell us what you want us to do. You want to split up, or are we doing all this together?"

"You can go with them if you want, Rachel," said Nana. "I'll straighten up here."

The list included picking up the dresses (and praying they'd all fit this time), checking on the cake, buying several paint pens at the craft shop, selecting gifts for the bridesmaids, and lastly a trip to the farmer's market for a watermelon and other fruit.

They were browsing in the gift shop, looking for something especially "Michigan-y" for the bridesmaids when Liz heard her sister chuckling.

"Hey sis," said Elaine." Check this out. Is this you, or what?"

Liz looked over at the plaque her sister was holding. It said:

> *"If you want to make God laugh,*
> *tell Him your plans."*

"Yep, that's me," Liz admitted. She wasn't sure she liked the idea of God's laughing at her frantic running around getting ready for one of the most important events of her life. But then, who was putting a gun to her head and ordering her to be frantic? With a twinge of guilt, she realized that she hadn't said anything to Him yet that busy day, much less tell Him her plans.

I'm sorry, Lord. Even saying something stupid would've been better than saying nothing. Just have Your way, OK?

There is a certain rush of peace that can come with surrender, as Liz remembered at that moment.

After a late lunch at the village coffee shop, the "girls" headed back to the cottage, where Nana had been cleaning and polishing the place until it sparkled. Bapa and George were sitting contentedly on the deck eating snacks and listening to the news through the screen door.

"George!" said Rachel the moment they'd reached the top of the steps. "What did the florist say?"

"He said all systems are go," George said without hesitation, apparently anticipating the all-important question.

"Thank goodness!" Rachel heaved a sigh of relief. George looked at her expectantly. "And thank you, too, dear," she added as if humoring a child.

"Ya done good, George," said Bapa, popping another pretzel into his mouth. The girls exchanged amused glances and began carrying in the fruit. Nana had cleared the kitchen counters, so Rachel began marking the watermelon for her swan carving, and Liz phoned Shannon.

"We're back! Meet us on the beach!" was all she had to say. George smiled at his daughters as they bounded down the steps toward the lake with plastic buckets, just as they had as little girls. Where had the time gone?

The air carried with it a cool hint of fall, but the lake was still warm from the August days, so the girls didn't mind wading in the water in search of smooth stones that were the right size and colors for their project. With the three of them it didn't take long to find the 120 they needed, but the day was so picture-perfect that they lingered, sitting on a long piece of driftwood, talking about the events of the day and discussing plans for the next day.

"I cut the tulle into little squares and the ribbon into pieces, so it shouldn't take us long to do the birdseed," said Shannon.

Elaine was puzzled. "Birdseed?"

"Instead of rice," Liz reminded her. "Exploding birds, remember?"

"Oh yeah, that's right."

"Thanks, Shannon," said Liz. "We got the paint pens today, so we're all set for the place markers, too. We can probably do them both in the morning ... right before the bridesmaids' luncheon." Liz smiled at the thought of all the fun coming up ... if she could keep from stressing out.

Just then Sean, Michael, and Pastor Dan came crashing through the trees and ran down the sandy ledge to where the girls were sitting. They stopped abruptly, sending a small shower of sand in their direction.

"Hey, watch it!" yelled Shannon, jumping up and brushing herself off.

"Sorry, kiddo," said Sean.

"What are you guys doing here?" Shannon asked.

"We're on a mission," said Michael cryptically. Seeing Elaine, he extended his hand. "Hi. I'm Sean's brother Michael," he said.

Elaine wiped the damp sand off her hand and shook his. "Hi. I'm Liz's sister—"

"—Elaine," Michael finished for her. "I've heard all about you."

"Great," said Elaine, giving her sister a wry look.

"So what's up, Michael?" Shannon asked again, seeing the hammer in her brother's hand and some long nails sticking out of his back pocket.

"Wouldn't you like to know?" Michael teased.

"We were just heading back anyway," said Liz, picking up one of the heavy buckets. Elaine got the other.

"What are those for?" asked Sean.

"Wouldn't you like to know?" Shannon replied, smirking at Michael and heading in the direction of the rented house. "I'd better go see if Mom needs help. See you guys later."

"See ya. Thanks for your help," said the other girls.

"That's right, rehearsal's at six o'clock," said Pastor Dan.

"—rehearsal dinner at seven!" Shannon called over her shoulder.

"Bachelor party at ten—woohoo!" said Michael. Sean laughed.

"Yeah, we'll drive on up to Bear Lake and have a really wild night on the town."

Liz and Elaine exchanged glances and snickered. "Yeah, the groomsmen can bury Sean in the sand up to his neck and throw night crawlers at him," Elaine quipped.

"What time is it anyway?" asked Liz. Elaine checked her cell phone.

"Four ten? We're doing better than I thought," she said.

"Actually it's five ten," said Pastor Dan looking at his watch. "That's odd."

Elaine held up her cell phone for better reception. "It's flashing back and forth between four ten and five ten. I guess it's four ten in Wisconsin."

"We'd probably better go," said Liz.

"Yeah, get outa here," said Michael. He seemed a little too eager to get rid of them, but the girls didn't have time to speculate.

"See you in an hour," said Liz, giving Sean a kiss on the cheek.

"The fruit is absolutely beautiful, dear!" Nana exclaimed as Rachel was sticking a blueberry eye onto the watermelon swan and using the toothpick to secure the head onto one of the wings. Rachel took a step back and seemed satisfied with the finished product. She took some plastic wrap, wound it several times tightly around the swan and its contents, and set it on a wooden tray.

"Hi Mom!" called Liz and Elaine as they burst through the door.

"We're back and headed for the showers," added Elaine. "Don't worry, we won't take long." Rachel looked at the clock.

"Oh my gosh, I'm not going to be ready on time!" she cried in frustration.

"Oh honey, you're not trying to catch a plane," Nana reassured her. "We've got all evening. You'll be fine."

"How about you, are you ready, Mother?"

"If this is OK for tonight," said Nana uncertainly.

"Oh sure, that'll be fine. It's going to be very casual," said Rachel.

"Well, now see? You can relax, dear. This isn't a race."

"But where in the world is George?" Rachel continued to fret.

"He and your father are helping the overflow cousins get settled into the motel and giving them directions to the beach and the O'Briens' cottage.—Oh, and Pastor Lambert called just before you got home. He's running a little behind—got into some construction around Chicago, but he'll be along soon. So see, you won't be the only one a little late." Her encouraging words didn't seem to be helping much.

"So, everything's under control … " Rachel began, but the moment she heard herself make the statement it sounded to her disturbingly like famous last words.

Twenty minutes later she had just turned on the shower when she heard the girls shouting to her. *Why must they wait til I'm running the water to try to talk to me?* she thought. She turned the water off.

"What did you say?"

"We said we're going to the O'Brien's. We'll meet you there, OK?"

"OK—Oh, girls, take the fruit salad in your car, OK?"

"OK. See you later!"

"'Bye." Hearing the sound of Nana's car pulling out, Rachel savored a moment of peace and quiet before turning the water back on. *It's almost over,* she told herself, letting the water pour over her head as if to wash away all the frustration and exhaustion.

Although she knew the St. Louis minister was also running late, she still felt it would be extremely rude for the mother of the bride to keep everyone waiting for half an hour. "Fashionably late" was one thing, "ridiculously late" was quite another. She hastily dressed, styled her hair as quickly as she could with a blow dryer and hairclip, dabbed on her makeup, and hurried to her car carrying just her purse and feeling as though she were missing something.

She started the car and headed slowly down the dune. When she got to the end of the driveway, she brought the car to a stop before turning onto the dirt road.

Thunk!

What in the world ... ? Rachel put on the emergency brake and jumped out of the car to see what she had hit. There was no large stone or branch or animal in the driveway, so she looked under the car.

So much for the hairdo, she thought as the clip came undone and her auburn curls fell into the dust. It was a wasted sacrifice, for nothing seemed amiss under the car, either. Puzzled, she got back in and slowly made her way down the road, listening for any other suspicious noises.

As she turned the corner onto the main road, she heard a gentle *thump!* coming from the vicinity of the back seat. She pulled over and looked back. That was when she spotted a familiar wooden tray, sitting on the back seat, minding its own business but conspicuously empty.

Oh great! Rachel fought back the tears as she wondered why in the world they would have put the swan in her car with no one to hold it. As it turned out, it was fortunate that she had wrapped it so tightly, for instead of scattering melon balls and grapes everywhere, the whole thing was just rolling around the floor like a football. Nana no doubt would have found this extremely funny, but Rachel did not see the humor at all. She sighed heavily, got out one more time, put the salad onto the tray, put the tray in the front seat, and continued to make her way down the road with one hand on the swan as if guarding a small child. She was not one who prayed spontaneously, but as she approached the rental cottage, Rachel silently asked, *Lord, would you please give me my mother's perspective?*

CHAPTER SEVEN

"Oh Rachel! That's gorgeous!" Colleen exclaimed as Rachel unwrapped the fruit. (*No thanks to some people!* Rachel thought, although Colleen's appreciation was helping disperse the ill feelings.) "Everyone, look at the swan Rachel made! Shannon, would you mind clearin' a spot in the middle of the table for this masterpiece?"

Her daughter dutifully rearranged the serving dishes on the buffet table, which was overflowing with salads and desserts and the hot pads that, along with the warm aromas coming from the kitchen, told everyone in the house that hot dishes were coming.

Pastor Dan and Dr. Lambert were in the den, getting acquainted and going over the order of the service. Although their styles were quite different, "grace" and "tolerance" ruled, and a well-balanced ceremony was in the making.

Liz introduced Sean's family and her maid of honor Sarah to Aunt Ellen and the Nashville cousins, Douglas and Bobby, along with their sister Amanda, her husband Tommy, and their five-year-old daughter Lilly and three-year-old son Hunter, who were the flower girl and ring bearer. Soon the conversation was flowing freely. Aunt Ellen and Colleen "hit it off" immediately and seemed to be kindred spirits as they finished the preparations for the dinner. Aunt Ellen would begin a sentence in her refined Southern dialect, and Colleen would finish it with a hint of Irish, and both ladies would laugh.

"Ladies and gentlemen," Pastor Dan announced, and the room became quiet. "It appears everyone is here, so I suggest we all make our way down the road to the beach before the food gets col—er, before it gets too dark." Everyone chuckled and headed for the door.

The site of the wedding was close enough that even the grandparents could walk, so the procession made its way down the dirt road to the beach.

Several railroad ties formed steps that made it a little easier for the ladies to get down the steep slope as the gentlemen held their hands to steady them. Amanda, who was already carrying Hunter, tried to take Lilly's hand, but the little girl wanted nothing to do with the steps. She gleefully ran down the little slope as if it were Merry Mountain, shrieking with delight, until her father took her hand firmly and gently said, "This way, cupcake."

Liz was keeping an eye on the steps, so it wasn't until she had reached the bottom that she looked up and gasped.

The altar and chairs had not been brought down yet, but the area had been raked clear of rocks and debris. The only thing that was set up was an eight-foot-tall cross made of two massive pieces of driftwood. With the evening sky over Lake Michigan it was a striking sight.

"Surprise!" said Michael, grinning.

"Wow ... " Liz murmured.

"You like it?" asked Sean.

"It's ... awesome," said Liz, who wasn't in the habit of throwing the word around like some but reserved it for things that were truly awesome; this was one of them.

Sean and Michael took sticks and drew lines in the sand to show where the altar and aisle would be. The ministers explained the order of the service and walked the wedding party through the stages. As Sean, Michael, Douglas, and Bobby stood with Pastor Dan and Dr. Lambert, down the "aisle" came Shannon, Elaine, Sarah, and finally Lilly, who seemed convinced that the flower girl was the most important person in the whole wedding. Hunter toddled beside her, holding the little sofa pillow his mother had borrowed for him to practice with.

"And finally, the bride and her father," said Dr. Lambert. George held out his arm to Liz, and as she took it he gave her hand a reassuring pat. After the madness and chaos of the past few days and the planning and preparations of the past year, suddenly the meaning of it all came over Liz in a flash flood of emotions. She was relieved that all the craziness was almost over. She was thrilled that at last she was going to be joined with the love of her life for the rest of her life. She was somehow sad that her father was getting ready to give her away, and she sensed his mixed emotions. Most of all she felt a profound gratitude for every person present, who had traveled so far to be with them for their all-important day: loving parents, devoted grandparents, free-spirited sister, and soon-to-be in-laws who were so cheerful and positive about going along with such non-conformist plans. She was grateful especially for friends like Sarah and of course Sean, both of whom had prayed for her while she was still lost. Most of all, as she looked up at the cross silhouetted against the evening sky, she was grateful for her Savior, who loved her enough to die so that she would never have to be alone in the darkness again.

"Well, that was a lovely party," said Rachel when they had arrived back at the cottage. "I think we should all get to bed, though. Tomorrow's a big day!"

"Gee, Mom, ya think?" Elaine asked, giving her sister a squeeze.

"Smart-aleck."

"I don't know if I can sleep tonight!" said Liz.

George and the grandparents didn't seem to have any problem with it, and they said their good-nights and disappeared down the hall. Elaine, Sarah, and Liz went back to the girls' room, but it was at least two hours before the chatter died down. Rachel, who was having a hard time sleeping herself, peeked in to see two out of the three girls sound asleep.

"You still awake, too?" asked the bride.

"Too much excitement for both of us, I guess," said her mother.

"Me too. I don't know if I'll ever get to sleep tonight, but I've got to!" Liz stressed.

Rachel sat on the edge of the bed. "Would you like me to play with your hair the way I used to when you couldn't sleep when you were little?" At the words "when you were little," Liz heard her mother's voice choke up, and tears of love filled her eyes.

"Sure, Mom, that'd be wonderful." She rolled over, and Rachel began to run her fingers through the long curls. Liz sighed with pleasure.

"That feels so nice ... hey Mom?"

"Yes, sweetie?"

"Sean said he liked the way my hair was, and that he wouldn't have liked it at all if I'd had it done in a fancy up-do. So that kinda worked out OK after all."

"He's got a point," her mother said unexpectedly "I guess out here something that formal might ... well, it might look odd on the beach ..." Rachel smiled, remembering the look on Liz's face when first hearing the quartet. "I guess things do work out even when they don't seem to," she said. "By the way, I think there was a misunderstanding about the watermelon swan tonight. You girls were supposed to take it with you."

"Oops, sorry ... Did it matter?"

"Well, kind of. I didn't know it was back there, and next thing I knew it was rolling around the back on the floor."

Liz gasped. "Really? Did it make a mess?"

"No, the Saran Wrap held it together."

"Wow, good wrappin', Mom."

"Well, dear, if I've learned anything from this wedding, it's to expect the unexpected."

"That is a good lesson in life," Liz agreed.

"And another thing, darling. You and Sean just keep tightly wrapped, and you'll make it through those bumps along the way." Liz couldn't remember a time when her mother had talked about life like this.

"Like you and Dad."

"Yes, like your father and me, Nana and Bapa, Aunt Ellen and Uncle Jack, you've had plenty of examples."

"I know. Don't worry, Mom. Sean and I are trusting God to … keep us tightly wrapped."

Rachel continued to play with the auburn curls until she thought that Liz was asleep. She bent over and gently kissed her.

"Thanks, Mom," said a sleepy voice. "Love you."

Rachel stopped in the doorway, mentally taking a picture to store in her memory for the years to come. "I love you, too, sweetheart," she whispered.

As Liz drifted off to sleep, she thought how fitting it was for the wedding to be taking place here, and in early September. It had always been a bittersweet time of year. The siblings, aunts, uncles, and cousins had always spent the last weekend of the summer taking family hikes in the woods, where the leaves were already starting to turn. They would be whistling the theme from "Bridge over the River Quai" in unison as they traipsed through the brush with walking sticks, trying with their hearty laughter to mask the melancholy that came from knowing that another summer had passed and they'd soon be going their separate ways.

But then another school year would start, with new friends, new teachers, new experiences, and Liz's attention would be focused toward the future. It was like this now. Tonight was her very last night as George and Rachel's little girl, Elizabeth Danfield. She had had precious few quiet moments lately, but when they came, she had found herself turning the pages of photo albums in her mind, cherishing the past. But now it was time to focus on the future; tomorrow she would become Mrs. Sean O'Brien.

And with a heart full of sweet memories and even sweeter dreams for the future, she drifted off to sleep … for a few hours, anyway.

CHAPTER EIGHT

Aunt Ellen awakened before the alarm, but instead of getting up right away, she lay staring at the patterns of light and shadow on the ceiling. She tried to say her morning prayers, but other thoughts were clamoring for her attention, and instead she found herself going over a mental checklist in anticipation of the reception later that day.

Amanda had helped her clean the entire house, backtracking repeatedly whenever the toddlers followed and undid their work; somehow it had all finally gotten done.

(Check.)

The neighbors next door had kindly offered to take Lilly and Hunter to the beach for a major portion of the day, allowing the adults to do some final preparations unhindered by the little helpers.

(Check.)

Between games with the toddlers, the "boys" (Douglas and Bobby) and Amanda's husband Tommy had taken care of the lawn, the gardens, the bushes, and the shutters; Tommy had even raked the beach.

(Check, check, check. check, and check.)

"Now all we need is a sunny day, Lord," Ellen murmured, turning her thoughts back to prayer. "Oh, please, Lord, make it nice for Liz and Sean."

Although everything seemed under control, she still felt she was missing something—or someone. With the recent focus on work, the atmosphere in the summer home was different from the usual magical, adventurous, unpredictable feeling of summers past.

"Oh, Jesus," she sighed. "I do miss Jack. He always made these special occasions such fun. I've been too serious about gettin' everything ready. He would have made a game out of it and had everyone laughin' ... " Even then, just picturing her late husband's face with that mischievous gleam in his eye made her smile. "He would've had so much fun with this," she mused. "He'd have some marvelous weddin' prank to play on everyone," she chuckled. Just then the alarm went off, and she got up to turn it off, having placed it at the far end of the room to keep herself from oversleeping. She pulled the curtain aside to see what the kind of day it was.

The scattered clouds that hovered over the lake still wore pink traces of the sunrise. Ellen took a moment to enjoy the beauty of the morning sky.

But then her gaze fell upon the yard, which looked distinctly different from the way it had looked a couple of days before, when Bobby had cut the grass.

What in the world—? she thought. Something uninvited was springing up all over the yard. She grabbed her robe and put it on as she quickly descended the stairs.

From the kitchen window Ellen got a better view of the volunteer crop. She had never seen weeds that looked like that in their yard before, yet there was something oddly familiar about them ...

Suddenly she realized what they were, recognizing the sprouts from her childhood days when she used to help tend the vegetable garden.

"Peas!?" She exclaimed. Just then she spotted a blue plastic pea shooter on the windowsill that served to confirm her suspicions.

"BOYS!" She called in a voice that managed somehow to be both dignified and no-nonsense. "Get up! Y'all have some pickin' to do!" She stared at the ridiculous sight as sleepy groans of protest came from the boys' bedroom.

Suddenly the bubble of seriousness burst, and she broke into uncontrollable laughter. As the tears streamed down her face, somewhere in the pink heaven of that morning, someone was chuckling along with her.

"Oh, Lord," she sighed when the giggles had subsided, "tell Jack I love him so!"

CHAPTER NINE

It was a wedding Liz had never planned or even imagined. The guests were all seated in the sand (The chairs had never arrived.) and not looking very comfortable, to say the least. The bridesmaids walked down the aisle with their hands in their pockets, since they had no flowers, and their hair was being whipped around by a strong wind. Four musicians came dancing out of the woods playing their instruments, which had mysteriously shrunk into tiny panpipes. Their legs had morphed into goats' legs, complete with hooves, and they had sprouted little horns. As if cued by the music, the "silly florist" came dancing in, shouting "The flowers are here!" and scattering red roses everywhere. He was so busy being a ham that he didn't see the giant cross but ran right into it, knocking it onto the altar, where a family of seagulls had built a nest. Lilly screamed, and as gull eggs scattered everywhere, one of the birds became tangled in Liz's hair. ...

Liz thrashed around until she woke herself up, entangled in the sheet that had come loose. She realized immediately that she had been dreaming, and she was very grateful. She looked at the clock and was not so grateful to see it was only 5:30, and there was very little chance she would get back to sleep. Every time she began to drift off, a little voice in her head (It must have been the florist's.) would say, *You're getting married today!* And the excitement would surge again. Finally she got up, trusting that the Lord and adrenaline would keep her going that day. There was still so much to do!

"Hey, bride lady," came Sarah's sleepy voice. "Are ya ready to hit the floor runnin'?"

"I don't know about that, but I'm excited. Sheesh! You wouldn't believe the dream I was having!"

"Ooo! Really? Tell me about it!" Sarah sat up, ready to hear a good story.

"Sorry, Sarah, it wasn't one of those God dreams ... at least it better not have been!"

"So you don't think He was trying to tell you something?"

"Probably not. ... Well, maybe he was trying to tell me I've been stressing out too much."

"You do need to trust Him more," Sarah agreed almost too readily.

"OK, I'll try."

"Anyone want to go to the beach, do some yoga, and start the day in peace?" Elaine had been eavesdropping. Liz and Sarah looked at each other.

"I'll go to the beach," said Liz evasively.

"Me too," said Sarah.

A short time later Elaine was doing salutations to the sun, casting long shadows over Lake Michigan while Liz and Sarah took turns reading Psalms and enjoying the freshness of the early morning. Autumn was definitely in the air, and a sudden chill in the wind caused Liz to glance up at the sky apprehensively. Her reaction did not escape Sarah's attention.

"It's OK, Liz," she said. "Trust Him." And she continued to read the words of confidence written thousands of years before. When she'd finished reading, the two girls walked the beach and prayed together. It was good to have a "prayer partner" to help shoulder the load and keep Liz's mind focused in the right direction in the midst of the whirlwind of activities and problems. Liz finally told Sarah about her disturbing dream, and they both had a good laugh.

Before they even reached the cottage they could tell Nana was up. The smell of coffee, bacon, and maple syrup floated down the sand dune like a breath of heaven.

"Nana, you're going to make us all fat," laughed Liz. "We need to fit into those dresses today."

"If my tux doesn't fit, I can always wear my Hawaiian shirt," said George who was already seated and helping himself to his third piece of bacon.

"Hey, that would work for me," said Bapa, who was also indulging.

"Dream on," laughed Nana. "It's a wedding, not a luau."

"It was worth a try," Bapa whispered to George.

"Thanks for fixing breakfast, Mother," said Rachel, who was buttoning her sweater as she came in. "My goodness! What a feast!"

"Well I hope you'll eat some," said Nana. "You've been going nonstop for days. You need to keep your strength up." She took more plates from the cupboard. "How many pieces of French toast would you like?"

"Three!" answered Bapa cheerfully.

"I wasn't asking you, I was asking our hard-working daughter. Here girls, you may help yourselves. Everything's ready."

Soon after breakfast Shannon joined the other girls on the deck to paint names on the stones they had collected.

"Good thing these 'place cards' aren't really cards," said Elaine as a gust of wind picked up the guest list and nearly carried it toward the lake. Sarah caught it and anchored it with two stones she had already painted. "These are a lot more practical."

Before long they had all the stones painted—the black ones with the male guests' names painted on in silver and the light grey ones with the female guests' names in black. Making sure the paint was dry, they put them in a shoebox to take over to Aunt Ellen's later.

Liz began to notice that the sky was getting darker and the wind was picking up. She didn't express her concern out loud, but the other three were exchanging wary glances.

"Are we getting some weather?" Nana asked, pulling the beach towels off the railing where they had been hung to dry. Liz's eyes met hers with an anxious look. Nana finished folding the towels and came over to give her a hug. As she did, she whispered some encouraging words to her. Then she went back into the cottage to finish straightening up. Liz could hear her humming "His Eye Is on the Sparrow," and she wondered if her grandmother was doing it for her benefit or if it was just what came naturally to her.

"Maybe we'd better do the birdseed inside," Shannon suggested, and the others agreed. Seeing Liz's worried expression, she added, "so we don't get attacked by birds out here."

Later, noticing the little sprinkles that had landed in the carpet, Sarah commented, "I guess we should've done the birdseed first—outside."

Rachel noticed, too, as she was on her way to buy more hairpins. She sighed with a conspicuous look of exhaustion and frustration.

"Go on, dear," said Nana, nudging her toward the door. "I'll vacuum when they're finished."

"Thanks, Nana," said Liz when her mother had left. She added when her grandmother was out of earshot, "I don't know what I'd do without her!"

"She has been sort of a stabilizing influence," Elaine agreed.

"What did she whisper to you when we were on the deck?" asked Shannon.

"'Be anxious for nothing,'" said Liz. "It's from the Bible."

"Ooo! I know that one! I memorized it at vacation Bible school years ago!" said Shannon. Her eyes always took on a certain sparkle whenever she was talking about Jesus or the Bible.

"'Be anxious for nothing,'" she quoted, "'but in everything, by prayer and petition, with thanksgiving, make your requests known to God. And the peace of God, which transcends all understanding, will guard your hearts and minds in Christ Jesus.'"

Sarah smiled at her enthusiasm. "Sounds like a plan to me," she said. As big drops of rain began pelting the windows, she added, "Maybe we should do that now."

They set down their work and joined hands for a prayer. It seemed pretty natural for three out of the four. It wasn't what Elaine was used to, but she went along with it willingly.

CHAPTER TEN

"So, if it's still raining tonight, what's the plan?" Douglas asked Sean. He and his brother Bobby, brother-in-law Tommy, and the O'Brien men had gathered at Aunt Ellen's to help set up for the reception.

"I guess the flaps come down on the tent to keep everyone dry," said Sean.

"What about the ceremony?" asked Bobby.

"It'll be in the tent, too," said Sean. "The head table will serve as the altar first, and we'll move the tables to make an aisle down the middle."

"So everyone will watch the ceremony from their tables?"

Just then Aunt Ellen's voice called from the kitchen, "Here comes the truck with the tent! Would you boys go and direct them please?"

"OK, Mom!" Douglas called back. "Let's go, guys."

They showed the delivery men around the house to the lake side.

"OK, let's get this thing up before the rain gets worse," said one delivery man, looking over his shoulder at the darkening sky.

It was difficult to set up the tent in the wind, but with eight men it was accomplished. They hastily took the tables and folding chairs off the truck and stacked them inside the tent.

"Where's the tablecloths and stuff?" Bobby asked.

"The caterer will bring all that in a bit," said Aunt Ellen, who had come outside to supervise. Just then her phone rang; she sighed and headed back into the house.

"Hello? ... Rachel, honey, what's wrong? ... Wait, slow down ... They what!? ... Oh no! ... Well, can't they get a hold of them? ... How in the world did that happen?—Well, never mind, it doesn't matter now. You just pull yourself together, dear, and try not to worry about it. ... It's gonna be all right, honey, don't you fret now. We'll think of something." She hung up the phone, turned, and saw six anxious faces.

"What now?" asked Michael.

"There's been a mix-up with the flowers."

"You have got to be kidding," moaned Sean. "What happened?"

"They blamed it on the computer, but it sounds like somebody gave it the wrong zip code, and that computer map thingy sent the delivery truck all the way to Onaway."

"Onaway to where?" asked Bobby, but no one was in the mood for joking.

"Where the heck is Onaway?" asked Douglas.

"Over three hours away. And they didn't realize the mix-up until they got there, which was when they should've been *here*. They aren't even going to try to get them here in time for the wedding." The men were ready to get back to work on the tables. Aunt Ellen, being the only female in the group, clearly was more upset about the situation than the "boys." However, Bobby was curious about the three hundred misdirected roses.

"So what happens to all those flowers?" he asked.

"The florist will probably just tell the driver to donate them to someone, drop them off at a hospital or church or something. If he has an ounce of sense, he won't drag the poor things all the way back here."

"Does Liz know about this?" asked Sean.

"I don't know, but Rachel's a basket case. I can't blame her—a weddin' without flowers?" She looked out at the tent. "*Now* what are we supposed to do?"

"I've got an idea!" said Douglas.

"Are you thinking what I'm thinking?" said Bobby.

"Let's go!" they both cried, and the others had nothing to do but follow as they disappeared around the house.

"Wait, boys!" called Aunt Ellen. "There are only two delivery men. Don't you think they'll want some help with the tables?" But if they had heard her, they were ignoring her. Pastor Dan alone accompanied her back to the tent.

"Today's been full of surprises," he said sympathetically.

And the next moment there was one more, as they heard the sound of a truck in the driveway.

"If that's the caterer, he's a bit early," said Ellen, glancing at her watch.

"Um, actually, it's the rental people," Pastor Dan observed. As they looked at each other, it took a moment for it to register what was going on, but by the time they broke into a run toward the truck, it was pulling away in the rain.

"WAIT!" screamed Aunt Ellen in a very uncharacteristic tone of sternness and desperation; even Pastor Dan was surprised. "You haven't set up the tables and ... chairs ... " She stopped breathlessly as the truck sped out of sight. For a moment she and Pastor Dan stood there, speechless and stunned. Finally, Ellen became indignant.

"Can you imagine?!" she sputtered. "They just drop them on the ground and leave?!"

"I guess we've got our work cut out for us," said Pastor Dan. "Hey guys!" he called. "Time to come and help with the tables!" The only answer was the sound of the rain on the tent. "Where do you suppose they went?"

"Oh, who knows?" said Ellen, who was getting more disgusted by the minute. "Well, Lewis and George are coming over soon. They can help us set up until those good-for-nothin' boys get back."

By the time Liz and the other girls arrived to place the stones around the tables, the three older men had set up most of them. The caterer had brought the linens and silverware and with the help of Aunt Ellen, Amanda, and Colleen, was following close behind, setting the tables as soon as they were set up. Everything seemed back on schedule. The tent was considerably smaller than the one originally ordered, which would have taken up the entire yard, so the way tables were set up was what Aunt Ellen called "cozy."

"I sure hope we don't end up having the ceremony in here," Pastor Dan thought out loud. "It'd be a tight squeeze."

The girls took a little longer putting the stones around, since Liz wanted to make sure all the guests were seated right where she wanted them. ("Picky-picky-picky," Sarah had teased.)

As they were laying out the last of the "place cards," Liz said, "Where are the centerpieces? Shouldn't they be here by now?" The older adults exchanged glances, and before anyone could stop him, Bapa blurted out, "Didn't your mom tell you?"

"Tell me what?" asked Liz, not certain she wanted to know the answer. That sinking feeling in her stomach was starting up again.

"The good news is, we aren't going to be charged a dime," said George brightly.

Ellen gave him a reproachful look, put an arm around Liz, and guided her toward the opening of the tent. "Don't you worry about that, honey. You just focus on getting yourself ready."

Liz looked around at the others, but clearly the older ones weren't going to tell her any more, and the younger ones were afraid to ask.

Ellen took both of Liz's hands and made sure she was making eye contact. Liz remembered that the last time she did that was days after her aunt had been widowed, the day Liz had found out Ellen knew Jesus.

"The Lord has everything under control," her aunt assured her. Liz wasn't quite convinced, as she fought back the tears.

How could I have planned this wedding for an entire year and still have everything go wrong?! she thought.

Suddenly she had a flashback of the plaque in the gift shop, and though at the moment she didn't find it at all humorous, and though her emotions were wrestling with being angry with God for letting all this happen, with her will she made the choice to let it go … or at least to try.

CHAPTER ELEVEN

As the girls approached the cottage, they could hear Rachel and Nana having an exchange. The words weren't quite intelligible at first, but Liz knew her mother was stressing, and Nana was trying to calm her down.

"Those *boneheads!*" fumed Rachel. "Wouldn't you think the florist or the delivery people or *someone* would think there's something a little bit odd about people three hours away ordering flowers from *Manistee*?!"

"The florist probably wasn't paying attention, and delivery people aren't paid to make judgments, dear, they're just paid to follow directions. I'm sure they've seen their share of strange things. You know the way some people plan their weddings these days. Some of them are downright peculiar."

"Don't I know it! Well, this is the craziest wedding I've ever been involved in! Maybe it'll be on the beach, maybe in a tent. No flowers … "

"There's no flowers?" Liz asked, confirming what she had already feared.

The women obviously hadn't heard them come up, and Rachel's demeanor changed abruptly.

"Oh honey, I'm so sorry," she moaned, her hand to her head as if trying to push back a migraine, and trying to think how to unsay what she was sure her daughter must have heard.

"But Sean called," Nana added hastily. "He didn't give me any details, but he said to tell you not to worry and to look up Philippians 4:19."

"Thanks, Nana," said Liz, trying hard to feel better about the situation.

When the girls got to the bedroom, it was clear that while everyone else had been busy that day, Nana had not been sitting around, either. The dresses were all hung neatly and flawlessly: Nana had steamed out every last hint of a wrinkle. The dresser had combs, brushes, hairspray, hairpins, elastic bands, curling irons, and Emory boards all carefully laid out, and on the bed was a first aid kit and sewing kit, fully equipped. It seemed Nana had thought of every possible kind of emergency that could come up, and Liz couldn't help thinking that whatever crisis hadn't happened yet, it was sure to happen before the end of the evening. (Or maybe Nana had anticipated Liz's thoughts and wanted her to feel prepared.)

"Look, Liz," said Sarah, pointing to her Bible on the nightstand. Nana had opened it to Philippians 4. Shannon picked it up and read,

"' … and my God shall supply all your needs, according to His glorious riches in Christ Jesus.'"

Remembering how beautiful the woodwind quartet had sounded, Liz smiled.

"I'm sure He will," she said confidently. Shannon and Sarah smiled back; Elaine was baffled but curiously optimistic.

"Rachel, the musicians have arrived," said George. "Do you want me to take them down to the beach?"

"Sure," said Rachel absently, pinning her hair for the third time.

"Where shall I have them set up?"

"I think they're supposed to be on the left."

"The left as you face the altar or facing away from the altar?"

"What?" said Rachel with thinly veiled irritation. " … Never mind, I'll come with you," she sighed.

"You look beautiful, honey," Nana reassured her.

Fifteen minutes later George and Rachel were standing at the edge of the sand with the four musicians.

"Do we still want to have this on the beach?" Rachel asked. The rain had stopped, but the sky was still dark and threatening.

"I haven't heard otherwise," said George. He went to the trunk to pull out the four folding chairs. "Look, the sky's getting a little lighter over the dune. I think the rain is moving west."

"I hope you're right," said Rachel.

"Hey, the wet sand is easier to walk on," George observed happily as he took the chairs down to the altar area.

The youngest musician was standing at the top of the slope, his instrument in one hand, music stand in the other. He had an odd look on his face.

"Is everything OK?" Rachel asked.

"Sure," he said, "as long as it doesn't start raining again." He stood staring at the beach as if something else were on his mind. Finally he turned to Rachel and asked, "Were you really planning on bringing a harp down there?"

"Well … that had been the original plan. Why?"

"Never would've happened," he said with a look of condescending amusement that Rachel found a bit annoying coming from a preteen.

"Really?" she asked.

He chuckled. "Even if you could get the van down here without getting it stuck in the sand, no way you could get a harp down here, at least not easily or safely," he said with authority.

"Really," Rachel repeated.

"Harps have to be moved on wheels over a flat surface. I suppose if you wanted to have about ten people carry … " He reconsidered, regarding the steep slope and shook his head. "Naaa … "

Rachel was still pondering the "would haves" as he and the rest of the quartet went to where George was and began to set up and go over their music. As her eyes followed him down, suddenly she saw it, and it fairly took her breath away.

The "good-for-nothin' boys" had been scouring the dunes and woods and vacant lots. Wildflowers were everywhere. They lined the sides of the sandy aisle. They were piled on the altar and strewn over the area in front of it. They hung from the cross in cascades of white, purple, and gold. Although they were a far cry from what had been planned, in this setting, with sand and water and sky, they were …

"Perfect," she whispered. She thought of the fretting she had done and the ill will toward the florist, which hadn't accomplished a thing. And now these wildflowers that had surrounded her daily, unnoticed and unappreciated, were not only utterly free, they were …

"Perfect," she murmured again, to no one in particular. She wasn't sure why tears filled her eyes at that moment, or how to describe how she felt, but she liked it. It was soothing yet exciting; it was mysterious, yet it gave her a sense of knowing, of sharing a private joke with a king.

It occurred to her that this might be what Liz called "a God thing."

CHAPTER TWELVE

September 8, 2001

Becca sat quietly in the back pew of the little church where she was to be married later that day. The altar was the epitome of simplicity. A vase stood with a solitary red rose, the symbol of their love. They had deliberately left the thorns on it to remind them of the hard times the Lord had brought them through. Behind the rose was a long, tapered white candle, waiting to be lit by two smaller candles on either side as a symbol of two lives becoming one.

Two such different lives, yet so alike in the things that had drawn them together. Both bride and groom were from highly orthodox families, but Becca's heritage was Jewish, Mosen's Islamic. Both had abandoned their childhood religions when confronted with the reality of the Living God and their Savior—"Yeshua" to Becca, "Issa" to Mosen, better known to most Americans as Jesus. Both had faced abject opposition from friends and relatives, accusations of blasphemy, threats, and eventually total rejection from their respective families. Becca's family considered her dead; Mosen's wanted him dead for the honor of the family.

Becca and Mosen's love for each other by itself would have been enough to make them outcasts. But they had been disowned before they had even met, and as it turned out, it was their status as spiritual refugees that had allowed them to find each other— and the proverbial silver lining. Thus, the symbol of their love was not only thorny but fragrant and beautiful.

The chapel was simple and, except for the rose, the candles, and a small cross, unadorned, much as their lives had become. There was no inheritance, no extended family, no home, except for a little apartment over a beauty shop.

This was certainly not the wedding Becca had dreamed of when she was a little girl. Those dreams had been full of music and laughter, hundreds of guests, and hundreds of flowers and candles. There would be vows spoken under a canopy, dancing and merriment that went on into the night, and the beginning of a life that would be a link in the eternal chain of their holy traditions.

She had never imagined that her wedding day would be like this—a humble minister and a few close friends that had become her new family, witnessing their vows in a tiny rural church. But neither had she imagined in her wildest dreams the kind of fulfillment she had found in her Messiah, who had already proven His love for her by offering up His own life as the ultimate atoning sacrifice to save her from death. It was a love she was still trying to fathom and probably would for the rest of her life. It was the kind of strength and self-sacrifice she saw in Mosen, her beloved. Though he had been forced to flee his home country, where the penalty for conversion was death, he counted it an honor to suffer for the One Who had suffered so much for him. An honor and a joy.

But sometimes Becca didn't feel the joy, like today. She didn't know if the lonely mood that threatened to suck all the pleasure out of her wedding day was sadness for herself—mere self-pity—or grief for her loved ones who were missing out on the wonder of salvation. They were waiting faithfully for the Messiah, and so often she had wanted to scream, "He's already come!"

Oh, Yeshua, open their eyes—please ...

"They say rain on your wedding day is good luck," a gentle voice spoke from behind her. She turned and smiled at the young man in jeans and a t-shirt.

"Pastor Stan! Hi." Although she hadn't intended it to, her voice betrayed the melancholy she had been fighting, and the minister's heart went out to her. He sat beside her, and for a moment all that could be heard was the drumming of the rain on the roof of the little church. They both sat looking straight ahead at the simple cross. Finally the pastor spoke.

"He's here, you know."

"Yes, Pastor, I know."

"And He will never leave you or forsake you."

Becca smiled. "Never has, never will."

"Becca, you've given up a great deal for Him. It hasn't gone unnoticed."

"I know. 'Great is my reward in heaven.'"

"Well, if my experience has taught me anything, I'd say you'll have some rewards here as well. Who knows? Your relatives may be pretending you don't exist, but believe me, they're watching you. And I suspect they already know that you've found something they don't have."

"I have," Becca agreed. "There's no comparison. They have their traditions; I have Him."

"Exactly. You know Him personally, and He knows you. Becca, He knows everything about you—how you feel, what you need, your dreams and desires. You've sacrificed for Him, but sacrifice isn't all there is to the Christian life."

"I know that," Becca said, as a surge of joy came over her. "He's given me Mosen. And you—Christian brothers and sisters, my new family … "

"And little things," the pastor promised. "They're all around you if you're watching for them—signs of His love. Things like a sunrise, a child's giggle, answers to your prayers coming from unexpected places, answers to prayers you haven't even thought to pray, those little surprises, … bursts of joy that seem to come from nowhere … "

"I know what you mean," said Becca, smiling. "I've had those."

"They're all His way of reminding you that He loves you. And He cares for you."

"Thanks, Pastor," said Becca, giving him a hug. "I always knew that, but I needed to be reminded. Well, I'd better go get ready." The pastor looked at his watch.

"OK. See you in a couple of hours." As Becca headed for the door, he added, "Watch for them."

"I know," Becca laughed. "The little things."

"Little things."

Imagine her surprise when an hour before the ceremony a truck arrived, delivering three hundred red roses, free of charge.

CHAPTER THIRTEEN

The Nashville cousins were wiping the rain off the last of the chairs when the guests started to arrive. The "boys" stashed their rags in the dune grass as the ushers began escorting the ladies to their seats, followed by the gentlemen, who glanced at their watches and the sky intermittently.

The quartet played its music, and the older guests were whispering to one another, obviously impressed (and some playing "Name That Hymn"), while the younger guests sat up straight and craned their necks to watch curiously.

Meanwhile, the wedding party was gathering. Pastor Dan, Dr. Lambert, and Sean quietly came from the woods to the north and joined the groomsmen to await their cue.

Liz, George, and the bridesmaids, along with the toddlers and their mother, lined up along the dirt road on the other side, hidden from the beach by the birch trees and one well filled-out evergreen. A minivan drove by slowly, the driver glancing out of the corner of her eye as several small children pressed their noses against the glass to stare openly.

"Thank You, Lord," Sarah murmured. "I wouldn't have thought of that."

"Thought of what?" asked Liz.

Sarah gestured with her thumb toward the minivan full of gawkers, which was just disappearing around the bend. "It just occurred to me that we would have had way more of that if the weather hadn't been so dreary all day."

"Wow, you've got a point ... Thanks, Lord."

Amanda's husband Tommy was handing the bridesmaids their bouquets. They were bunches of delicate wildflowers in white, gold, and deep purple.

"Oooo! Pretty!" Lilly squealed with delight, her eyes like blue saucers. The others agreed that the early autumn flowers complemented the bridesmaids' purple dresses perfectly.

"I hope nobody's allergic."

"Thanks, Tommy, these are beautiful," said Liz, turning hers curiously to see how it had been tied together.

"Oh, by the way," Tommy chuckled, "Sean's grandfather would want you to know he made some sacrifices for these. Most of his fishing line is spent."

"I'll have to remember to thank him."

The music had stopped, and the musicians looked up at the ushers to see if everything was ready. The ushers looked over to where Pastor Dan was signaling them that they were in position. They looked up through the trees to see if the ladies were all set as well. Seeing what was going on, Lilly took it upon herself to get this show started.

"We're ready!" she yelled before her mother could cover the little mouth. A warm wave of laughter swept through the congregation of friends and family, and the musicians began the processional. Rachel, Colleen, and Nana were ushered to their seats of honor, followed by Bapa and Sean's grandfather. The ministers came out with the other men, who each had a sprig of white and purple in his lapel.

"OK, Shannon, it's show-time," Liz whispered to her soon-to-be sister-in-law. Shannon grinned and started down the aisle, met with smiles and murmurs of approval. Someone on the bride's side whispered, "The groom's sister," and someone else whispered, "Lovely!"

Elaine was next to go, after one last sisterly hug. Sarah, next in line, turned to Liz and mouthed the words "I love you!" Liz mouthed "Love you, too!" and Sarah was on her way.

Amanda was down on one knee, softly giving her children one last reminder to walk slowly and quietly to where the others were standing.

"We *know*, Mama!" said Lilly impatiently.

"Sh! No talkin' now," she reminded them one last time. "OK, go."

They toddled down the aisle dutifully and were halfway to the altar when Amanda took a step and almost fell over something in the sand. Looking down, she saw Lilly's brand new, just-for-the-weddin' shoes, left behind. She and Liz smiled at each other and shook their heads.

"OK, sweetie," said George. "Let's do this." He held out his arm to her, and Liz took it, impulsively kissing him on the cheek.

"I love you, Daddy," she whispered. George didn't dare try to reply, and the song changed just in time to keep them both focused.

The guests were standing, each looking back and smiling at Liz—all but Nana. She had the habit of watching the groom instead. She always figured she had all evening to see the bride's dress, but she had one chance to see that look on the groom's face the moment he saw his bride appear, and she didn't want to miss it.

As usual, there was a detail that Nana caught which the others would miss. As the bride was being escorted his way, Sean's eyes glistened for a moment, and she saw his lip quiver. A split second later, he regained his composure, and the moment was gone, captured only in Nana's memory.

As George and Liz reached the altar, Sean looked as if the next little puff of wind would knock him over. As it was, the next bit of breeze parted the sky, and the sunshine they had waited for all day finally arrived. Bapa looked up at the sky.

"Well, what'd'you know?" he whispered. "The sun's out."

"I know," said Nana whispered back smugly. "I prayed."

"Good job," said Bapa, impressed, giving her hand an affectionate pat.

"Who giveth this woman to be joined to this man?" Dr. Lambert asked.

"Her mother and I do," George announced loudly, dutifully including his wife in the transaction.

Liz's hand was passed from George to Sean, and her father gave her one last kiss as his little girl and sat down with his wife.

"Dearly beloved," Dr. Lambert began in his usual ecclesiastical voice that seemed slightly out of place on the beach, but soon it softened as he appeared more relaxed.

There was a sense of God's presence that grew stronger as the ceremony progressed, felt by each person in a different way.

Lilly, who wasn't excited by any grownup talk, much less ceremonial grownup talk, wiggled her toes contentedly in the sand, somehow sensing that all was well with the world and that she had permission just to be a child and enjoy the love that was in the air.

Hunter, sensing the same thing, had sat down on his little pillow, figuring what was it for if not for that? He sat quietly and happily, making miniature roads in the sand and driving little stone "cars" down them. Amanda, who had slipped in the back after Liz and George, watched the children like a hawk at first, but eventually sensed that they were being watched and managed by Someone who had their best interest at heart and that she was not to fret today.

It was clearly raining in other places, evidenced by a rainbow that appeared as Pastor Dan was speaking about the goodness of God's promises, and Dr. Lambert stood gazing at it in wonder. The youngest musician was wide-eyed as well, having lost his cockiness with the sudden appearance of the sun.

Seeing their faces, Rachel glanced behind her and was awestruck. That feeling she had loved came to her again, a privileged feeling of knowing something beyond mere surface facts. It finally occurred to her that God hadn't sent the clouds and rain to personally torment her and cause anxiety. He was the Master Wedding Planner, (Liz would have said He was the Director of the show.) and these were a part of the scenery, a unique backdrop for a unique (She had said "crazy.") wedding.

As Liz and Sean were taking their vows, the sun seemed to shine more brightly, and by the time they were exchanging rings it was brilliant, radiating off the flower-decked cross and Liz's white gown. The photographer was finding that the constantly changing light presented some challenges, but that it also gave him a chance to take some spectacular photos. In his excitement he felt a momentary surge of pride at the masterpieces he was creating. But then he was struck with a sudden unspoken rebuke of humility in the realization that he had created none if this; he was merely photographing it.

Aunt Ellen and Beverly Walker, both recently widowed, felt the presence of their beloved husbands along with the presence of the God their men had loved. Rather than envying the happy couple or indulging in self-pity, these two were basking in the inner glow of joy that came with the anticipation of the great reunion that lay ahead.

Nana was still thinking about the overwhelming elation she had seen on Sean's face upon seeing his beloved as his bride after waiting for her for five years. As she remembered that moment, her Lord was speaking to her about His love for *His* bride—the Church.

Did you see the joy on the bridegroom's face? she heard Him say in her heart. *He feels that joy after waiting for his beloved bride for just a few years. Can you imagine how I long for My Bride, and the joy she will bring Me after I've waited for her for thousands of years?*

This time it was Nana's lip quivering.

As for Liz, after so many months of planning and preparation, she expected each moment to pass distinctly, almost in slow motion. As it was, everything seemed to happen at lightning speed, yet there were details that would be etched in her memory for the rest of her life. The feeling of her father's soft kiss and the trace of a tear that it left on her cheek. The momentary appearance of the rainbow, like a wink from God.

The Band-Aid on Sean's thumb that she hadn't seen until they were exchanging rings. (Apparently he had sustained some kind of injury putting up the cross.) Most of all there was the fleeting yet profound thought that her other Bridegroom had much deeper scars of love on His hands, and that He was there.

He was unmistakably there.

CHAPTER FOURTEEN

Afterward, when all the group photos had been taken, the wedding party was ready to head for the reception. They were discussing who would go in whose car when they heard a horn honking. "The boys" pulled up in a Dune Buggy that was covered with white crepe paper streamers fluttering in the breeze.

"The bride and groom go with us!" declared Douglas.

So Liz and Sean got to ride in style. Although admittedly it was a bumpy ride, it was "the scenic route." They bounced their way over the dunes as the sun peered through the clouds on the horizon, setting the whole sky aglow.

"Are we going the right way?" Liz shouted over the sound of the Dune Buggy, the wind, and the waves. The route to Aunt Ellen's was around the smaller lake to the "south side," and yet they were bouncing along the dunes toward the channel; Liz could see the flashing of the lighthouse.

"Trust us!" Douglas shouted back, and Liz looked at him skeptically. These were the same cousins that had once missed their plane because they had been sidetracked in the airport arcade. Then after rescheduling, they had actually missed their second flight for the same reason.

We're supposed to trust them ... she thought, not quite convinced.

When they had almost reached the channel, they turned and headed through the public access area to the road that connected the Lake Michigan beach to the smaller lake. They stopped at a tiny building marked "Yacht Club." It resembled a yacht club about as much as a Chihuahua resembles a great Dane; it was about the size of a large garage with a fenced in yard containing a shuffleboard court, a sand box, a volley ball net, and a flagpole.

"Lord and Lady O'Brien, your yacht awaits you!"

There, bobbing alongside the solitary little dock was the Jacksons' fishing boat, all decked out for the occasion. A canopy of chicken wire was attached with bamboo poles stuck in the gunwales. Wildflowers and fluttering crepe paper streamers were woven into the canopy, and while Liz and Sean were staring and taking it all in, Bobby jumped out of the Dune Buggy, ran over to the boat, and began lighting some of the sparklers that had been duct-taped to the sides. Although he only lit every third one, the effect was quite stunning. Impressive, that is, for a tiny aluminum boat affectionately nicknamed the "Ocean Liner" by the Jackson boys.

The motor was only about 5 HP, so it took a while for the ship to putter across the lake to Aunt Ellen's. Liz wondered if Sean was wondering what kind of strange family he had just married into, but she smiled to herself, thinking that whatever he thought, it was too late for him to turn back now.

By the time they approached the reception, the sparklers had all fizzled out, so Bobby again lit every third one. They could hear the sound of happy voices emanating from the yard as they approached the dock. Douglas shouted, "Ladies and Gentlemen, Mr. and Mrs. Sean O'Brien!" The couple was met with applause and cheers, and the party began filling up the little tent.

The inside seemed somehow bigger. It glowed with dozens of votive candles, swiped from Aunt Ellen's stash and scavenged from every store in three villages. Each table contained an old fashioned Coke bottle with a spray of wildflowers. The painted stones marked the places, but each table was also strewn with several pieces of brown, green, and clear beach glass, collected by Aunt Ellen for the past thirty years and swiped by the boys from the large jar on her mantle.

The sides of the tent had been left open for the most part, and there was just enough breeze. Looking out, one could see the stars, the dunes, and the distant lights from the little town, reflected in the lake. Friends of the family who had traveled from St. Louis, Nashville, and Chicago were enthralled at the beautiful setting. Most of these people were the country club set, not used to traipsing through the sand to attend a wedding or seeing the bride and groom arrive at the reception, windblown, in an aluminum boat decorated with chicken wire and weeds, but the word "unique" came up several times, "beautiful" more, and "perfect" most of all. One of Rachel's friends whose name was Barbara fairly gushed her approval.

"Oh Rachel!" she cried. "I have never been to such an *extraordinary* wedding! Everything is so … so *unique* and *quaint* and *beautiful*. The ceremony was *so* moving!

I don't know when I've felt so … so … moved," she stammered. "I just can't find the words … it was absolutely perfect."

"Thank you, Barbara," said Rachel. She knew this woman could be a flatterer at times, but she somehow could sense that this was not one of those times. If she was feeling half of what Rachel was feeling …

"I mean it, dear. It was perfect. I don't know how you pulled it off way out here. To have everything planned so perfectly… "

Rachel couldn't help it; she burst out laughing. "Actually, Barbara, practically nothing went as planned … as *we* planned," she added thoughtfully. "But it was perfect … " Her voiced trailed off, and there it was, that feeling again. Rachel felt sure Barbara must have sensed it, too, because when their eyes met, Rachel saw that her friend's were misting up as well.

As with the wedding, the reception flew by all too quickly. Liz wished she could slow things down so she could take it all in. The faces of the dear friends that had traveled so far, like Beverly Walker, who was practically like another mother to her in her Chicago home. Liz made a point of introducing her to Aunt Ellen, and now she was pleased to see them sitting together like old friends. They were giggling and talking, obviously about things other than their recent widowhood, until Sean's grandfather asked if there was going to be dancing at this party or not?

Ellen replied that there could be if someone would help her get out the "Victrola." Grampa obliged, and Ellen got her "boys" to dig out the old heirloom records. With Liz and Sean's permission, they put on some of the Swing music from the 1940's. Instantly the portion of the yard not covered by the tent became the dance floor. Nana and Bapa, Sean's grandfather and Aunt Ellen's fun-loving mother started the dancing and were soon joined by the twenty-something set, who had picked up Swing at college during the retro craze; the Woodstock generation looked on in awe, and the teenagers present added "random" to the list of adjectives describing the evening.

Before they knew it, the couple was leaving in the same boat they had arrived in, with the remaining sparklers lit. They shook the birdseed out of their clothes and gave one last wave to the well-wishers, who then went back to dancing on the green "dance floor" (made possible by the cozy seating in the too-small-just-right tent that was not the one they had ordered.) "into the wee hours of the mornin'," as Colleen later recounted.

"I can't believe your cousins didn't think to get enough gas in the boat!" Sean grumbled half kiddingly as they were finally in the car heading for Traverse City.

"If you think running out of gas was an accident, you don't know my cousins very well yet," said Liz, trying hard not to laugh too much. "Didn't you see the look on Bobby's face when he apologized and handed you the oar? He never was a very good actor."

"Well, all I can say is, it's a good thing we aren't trying to catch a plane tonight. We never would've made it. You were right to have me book it for tomorrow night instead."

"Wow, we've been married four hours and you're already admitting I was right about something?"

"Yeah, well, don't let it go to your head."

"Well, I had a feeling, knowing those guys, that something would hold us up. Besides, Traverse City's a great place to spend a day in transition. If we went right from the boonies to the Big Apple, think what a shock that would have been!"

"You've got a point," Sean admitted.

"Besides," he added, giving her a look that gave her chills, "I really don't want to spend our wedding night on a plane."

PART II

"Are not five sparrows sold for two pennies? Yet not one of them is forgotten by God. Indeed, the very hairs of your head are all numbered. Don't be afraid: you are worth more than many sparrows."

—Luke 12:6-7

CHAPTER FIFTEEN

September 9, 2001, 9:15 PM EDT

As the Sunday night flight approached New York City, the steady drone of the plane was broken by the sound of a familiar voice.

"Hey, Mrs. O'Brien," said Sean, giving Liz a gentle nudge. "Wake up and get a look at the Big Apple."

Liz opened her eyes, gave her husband a sleepy smile, and turned toward the window. "Oh my gosh!" she gasped. "It's beautiful!"

The movement of the plane gave an extra dimension to the dazzling sight below—skyscrapers of various sizes and shapes, millions of lights sparkling as far as one could see, the Statue of Liberty bathed in light, and the World Trade Center behind her like literal pillars of the free world. It was breath-taking. Liz watched the scene for a few minutes, mesmerized.

"Where's Broadway?" she asked.

"I'm not sure," said Sean. "But don't worry, we'll find it," he added.

They had to find it. They had tickets for four shows.

September 10, 2001, 7:00 AM EDT

Liz awakened to the sound of the hotel room door shutting.

"Sean?" she called hoarsely, but obviously he hadn't heard her. She wondered where he was going, but her curiosity was not enough to induce her to move from the king-size bed, which felt so luxurious that she decided just to enjoy the freedom of not having to rush off anywhere. For a while she just stretched out in the acres of satin sheets and took in the beauty of the surroundings. The high-ceilinged room was decorated with sophistication, with paintings in gilded frames and satin cushions on the loveseat. Multiple layers of drapes hung over the high windows in elegant patterns. Fresh flowers in a crystal vase on the dresser filled the room with their fragrance. Liz noticed reflected in the full-length mirror on the bathroom door that there was even an orchid in a vase by the sink, along with ornate little bottles of any toiletry one could possibly need. Liz sighed with contentment. She stretched lazily, and her arm touched a piece of paper on Sean's pillow. Taking it, she smiled to see in his handwriting his new favorite name for her.

> Good morning, Mrs. O'Brien!—Glorious morning!
> I have gone for a run in Central Park. I'll see you in a little bit.
> Love,
> Mr. O'Brien
>
> P.S. If you're hungry, feel free to call room service for breakfast. Mine can be coffee, juice, and muffin—or surprise me.

Finally Liz got up, opened the drapes, and looked out at Central Park. It was a beautiful morning, but was Central Park a safe place to run? Having grown up in St. Louis, she remembered that her parents had always been adamantly against her going into Forest Park alone. She remembered hearing about crimes committed there, but she also knew her parents had a tendency to be overly protective, especially when it came to their youngest daughter. Now that their youngest daughter was in New York City, which was completely unfamiliar to her, she wasn't sure what to think. She had certainly heard of the city's crime rate and crimes taking place in Central Park, but maybe those were just at night. It was hard to imagine anything bad happening on a glorious day like this.

"So how was Central Park?" Liz asked when Sean returned. She had already showered and dressed and was brushing her hair at the dressing table.

"Beautiful!" he panted. "Lots of people there with the same ideas—running, walking, biking ... "

"So it's safe?" she confirmed. Sean looked slightly amused.

"Of course," he reassured her. "In the morning especially. There are a lot of people out, the police are riding around on horseback. You can even get a carriage ride."

"How romantic!" said Liz. "Could we do that sometime while we're here?"

"Sure," said Sean. "If you don't think it's too dangerous … " he teased.

"OK, OK," Liz laughed sheepishly. "I don't mean to be turning into my mother. I just want you to be safe. If you insist on running every day, just stay on the main paths, where there are plenty of people, OK?"

"OK. I promise."

"In fact, promise me that while we're in New York we'll stick to places with lots of people—No short cuts through the alley, no moonlight walks off the beaten path."

"Yes Ma'am," he promised. "Today we're taking that group sightseeing tour of Ellis Island to see Lady Liberty and all. Tomorrow we're going to visit my Uncle Phil in the World Trade Center, where about fifty thousand people work. Is that safe enough for you?"

"Perfect," she said with a smug grin.

"We'll be having breakfast at Windows on the World," he added.

"Is that part of the complex?" Liz asked.

"It's at the top of the North Tower—Uncle Phil's building—on the 106th and 107th floors."

"The what?!" Liz gasped. "I've never been on floor with a triple-digit number before! It'll be like eating on an airplane!"

"A low-flying plane, but without the noise. And the view is spectacular! Tomorrow's supposed to be a clear day, so we'll be able to see all of Manhattan—the Empire State Building, the Chrysler Building, or the Statue of Liberty … depending on what we're wearing," he laughed.

"What do you mean?"

"When I was there before, I didn't realize there was a dress code. I wasn't wearing a jacket, so we couldn't get into the restaurant. They seated us at the bar instead. Uncle Phil didn't mind, though. He said he had done the same thing. Only that time the maitre d' was nice enough to lend him a jacket."

"Really? That doesn't sound like New York City. More like small town friendly."

"Well, you can find nice people anywhere, if you're looking," said Sean. "New York is full of nice people."

"A hundred and six floors …" Liz was still trying to fathom the altitude of the place. "How much time should we allow for getting there? If the elevator stops at every floor …"

"Oh, they've got a cool system," said Sean. "If you're not going to one of the first

42 floors, there's the Skylobby Express elevator that'll take you non-stop to the 43rd floor. Then you can go on from there on one of the 'local' elevators."

Liz thought about this for a moment.

"Or," she suggested, "we could take the stairs all the way up, and you can skip your morning run in the park."

Sean chuckled.

"In that case, we'd have to call Uncle Phil and tell him we'll be meeting him for *dinner*."

Eight hours later they were returning from a full day of sightseeing.

"New York is cool, but it's exhausting!" Liz exclaimed, collapsing onto the king-size bed. Sean laughed.

"Especially when you cram two days' worth of sightseeing into one day," he added, flopping next to her.

"I'm starved! What are we doing for dinner?"

"Not much, if we're going to make it to the theater on time."

"—Oh! You're right! … doggy bags?"

"Works for me."

So the newlyweds raided the little refrigerator in their room. The leftovers from the late-night supper the night before made a small and somewhat messy meal, but the way they savored every bit of it, one would think it was a champagne dinner at the Ritz.

CHAPTER SIXTEEN

The phone startled Rachel awake the Tuesday morning following the wedding. It was 6:45, but after the twelve-hour drive home the day before, she had expected (and hoped) to sleep in a little longer before hitting the coming-home tasks of unpacking, mail sorting, and grocery shopping.

"Hi Mom!" came the cheery voice on the other end, and Rachel realized immediately that it was her daughter the bride.

"Elizabeth!" she exclaimed, trying to sound awake, but the hoarseness in her voice gave her away.

"Oh, I'm sorry, did I wake you up?"

"It's OK, honey. It's almost 7:00, and I have a lot to do, so I probably needed to get up anyway."

"Almost *seven* o'clock?! Oh, I'm sorry, I completely forgot about the time difference!" Liz apologized again.

"Oh, that's OK, honey," Rachel reassured her again, realizing what a rare privilege it was for a mother-of-the-bride to get a call from her daughter on her honeymoon—unless … "Is everything all right?" she asked.

"Oh sure. I'm just waiting for Sean to get back from his morning run and thought I'd give you a call." Liz's voice sounded upbeat and breezy.

"So how's the honeymoon so far?"

"Amazing, Mom! We saw *Phantom* last night, and it was *awesome*! You and Dad have seen it, haven't you?"

"Actually, we were going to, but we got called back early when Nana had her heart attack."

"Oh, I remember that trip. Too bad it was cut short. Well you guys need to see *Phantom* sometime, it's incredible! The music is gorgeous, and the special effects are so … so … "

"Special?" Rachel guessed.

"Yeah, I guess that's the word," Liz laughed. "At the beginning this huge chandelier sort of floats in over the audience and crashes on the stage. Then later they have this scene change where the set for the sewers rises up in all this mist, and … as I said, you have *got* to see it!"

"So what's on the schedule today?"

"We're meeting Sean's Uncle Phil for breakfast at a place called Windows on the World at 8:30. It's at the top of the World Trade Center."

"Now *that* I have done!" said Rachel, who was awake by now. "Spectacular view! I hope you have a clear day."

"We do. It's gorgeous."

"You'll love it! What time did you say you were going?"

"We're supposed to meet him at 8:30—wow, that's soon! I guess I'd better go. My battery is about shot anyway."

"Have a wonderful time, honey."

"Thanks. We will. Love you! Say hi to Dad for me."

When they had said their good-byes, Rachel lingered in bed in a state of adrenaline letdown, thinking about the day ahead. There was much to do, but Rachel allowed herself some moments of self-congratulation. Although the stress and excitement of planning a wedding had been draining, the finished product had been more than worth the effort. The wedding day itself had passed in a whirlwind of longtime friends, reunited family, meeting new family, rituals, traditions, toasts, and dramatic entrances and departures. But now that the stress and uncertainty was over, the most interesting thing on Rachel's agenda was seeing the proofs of the pictures the photographer had taken. She did look forward to seeing the photos. But what would they do for excitement now?

About an hour later, Rachel and George were finishing breakfast on the patio, lingering over coffee and talking about the wedding and their plans for the day.

"Don't forget, George, the tuxedos have to be back by noon."

"Roger," her husband replied, all business.

Rachel started to take a sip of coffee, but stopped short with her cup frozen in mid air. "Do you hear the phone?" she asked.

"Let the machine get it," said George, enjoying the peacefulness of the yard. Besides the faint ringing from the kitchen the only sound was the buzzing of a hummingbird that flitted around a hanging basket of geraniums. Rachel hesitated and then put her cup down.

"No, I'd better get it. It might be the photographer," she said, pushing away from the table. At the scraping sound of her chair, the hummingbird vanished.

As she hurried into the house, George gazed out at the yard, assessing the condition of the landscape. The teenager he had paid to do the yard work had been there, but he had not done the kind of meticulous job George would have done himself. He began making a mental list of what needed to be done.

Re-trim the hedges, weed-whack around the trees, …

A shriek from the kitchen interrupted his train of thought. It was Rachel.

"George! Come quick!" George sprang from his chair, knocking it to the ground with a clatter.

Bursting into the kitchen, he found Rachel with her eyes glued to the screen of the TV in the corner. Her face was ashen, her lips trembling, her eyes filling with tears. She instinctively reached for his hand.

"What's going on?" George asked, staring at the image of a smoking skyscraper. Suddenly his eyes widened. "Is that the … "

"World Trade Center. Yes! George, the kids are there!"

"Now? Are you sure?" George gasped, feeling the blood drain from his face.

"Elizabeth just called about an hour ago. She and Sean were meeting Sean's uncle for breakfast at the Windows on the World. It's at the very top of that tower!"

"Are you sure they're in that one? Could they be in the other tower?"

"No, I'm sure," Rachel replied miserably. "I remember when we were there. Remember, we went to the South Tower by mistake and went up about fifty floors before realizing we were in the wrong building?" Other times they had recalled that misadventure they would share a laugh; not today.

"Maybe they haven't gotten there yet … Did Liz say what time they were meeting?"

"She said 8:30."

George looked at his watch and sighed with relief. "Honey, it isn't even 8:00 yet."

"It's almost *nine* o'clock in New York!" she screamed. The tension had been building, and now the dam burst and the tears started. George enfolded her in his arms, and she wept into his shirt. "The plane hit at 8:47," she sobbed.

"They'll be Ok, honey," George tried to reassure her. "If the elevators aren't working, they'll just have to stay put until the fire is put out. They'll have an exciting story to tell their children someday." He tried to laugh, but that was too much of a stretch. "They might even have been running late ... you know Liz." He tried again to laugh, but he was finding that his breath was coming in shallow gasps. *This can't be happening!* he thought. A freak accident like this, on the one day his daughter was ... but airplanes didn't fly right over Manhattan! This had to be a very bad dream.

The couple stood holding onto each other, staring at the screen, and waiting for the nightmare to end.

CHAPTER SEVENTEEN

September 11, 2001, 7:57 AM CDT

Nana, still in her robe, poured her first cup of coffee and sat down at the kitchen table with her Bible. She sighed serenely as she read the verses of Psalm 91. She knew these words by heart, but this morning it was a pleasant bit of serendipity to come across them again. Nana had read the Bible cover-to-cover countless times, sometimes straight through in a year, sometimes more, sometimes less. She tended to go though the Psalms more slowly, savoring the ones she knew by heart, pausing at verses that had inspired hymns she knew, to remember the rest of the words, and maybe even sing the hymns if her voice was up to it. Her Bible was worn and underlined, with hand-written notes filling the margins.

"God's protection" was written at the top of this Psalm, and as Nana read the words encouraging the child of God not to worry or be afraid, she smiled, remembering how He had taken care of everything pertaining to the wedding, in spite of Liz and Rachel's fretting. He had provided beautiful music that fit the setting and surrounded them with gorgeous substitutes for the roses that had gone astray. He had given them perfect weather—raining enough all day to keep the boaters away, clearing in time for a moving ceremony, complete with rainbow. He had even kept Liz from wasting time and money on a hairdo that Sean wouldn't have liked anyway.

Nana closed her eyes, happily remembering the way the bride's and groom's faces had glowed as they were saying their vows, and later as they were leaving the rustic setting of the reception, heading for their honeymoon in the Big Apple.

Thank You, Lord!

The phone rang next to her, but she knew her husband was up. He could get it in the bedroom. She began her prayer again but was again interrupted.

"Flora!" She was startled by the stress in his voice. Bapa was ordinarily so easy-going. She had rarely seen him get rattled so quickly.

"What is it?" she called. Bapa was in the living room turning on the TV.

"That was George on the phone. He said to turn on the TV."

The moment she stepped into the living room Nana knew something was horribly wrong. Not able to find the remote control and not wanting to take the time to search for it, Bapa was down on one knee, manually flipping through the channels to get the news station he preferred. But it didn't seem to matter. Every channel had a variation of the same picture—the image of twin skyscrapers, one pouring out smoke into the blue sky of an otherwise beautiful morning.

"Lew, what's happening?!" Nana cried.

"Bad fire in New York City—plane crashed right into the World Trade Center," he said. His eyes never left the screen, and his face registered shock and horror. "How crazy is that?"

"A small plane did that?"

"Not a private plane. It was a regular commercial airline." Bapa's voice sounded strange and far away, and Nana tried to dismiss the sense of foreboding that closed in like a gathering storm.

"That *is* strange … I hope Liz and Sean aren't anywhere near that."

Bapa's head snapped up, and something about the way his eyes met hers gave Nana a stabbing pain in her chest.

"They are, Flora. They're on the top floor."

"So … " Nana began, suddenly short of breath, "how long will it take to put the fire out?"

Before Bapa could answer, an even more bizarre sight hit them like a thunderbolt; another plane flew into the second tower, sending out another giant fireball. And as flashbacks of World War II descended on them without warning, they both knew immediately that this was no accident; this was an act of war.

Nana sank into the armchair. "Oh Jesus!" she cried. "Please get them out of there!" Then as if grabbing for a life preserver she began speaking the verses she had just read.

"If you make the Most High your dwelling
—even the Lord who is my refuge—
then no harm will befall you,

no disaster will come near your tent.
For he will command his angels concerning you ... "[1]

---

[1]Psalm 91:9–11

CHAPTER EIGHTEEN

September 11, 2001, 6:32 AM PDT

Rick had been vaguely aware that the phone was ringing and that Elaine was answering it and getting up, but he had gone right back to sleep for a few minutes. Now with the California sun peeking through the drapes he was aware that she was still not next to him, and the TV was on in the living room. He reached for his glasses and looked at the clock: 6:32. *What's Elaine watching so early in the morning?*

He rolled over and closed his eyes, but moments later his curiosity won out, and he staggered from the bedroom to see what had gotten his girlfriend up and captured her attention at such an hour. The image on the TV of twin towers in flames seemed surreal.

"Sci-fi Channel?" he asked, although the moment the words were out he recognized the somber voice that was announcing an attack on the World Trade Center and realized that what he was seeing was very real. Elaine ignored the question.

"Mom called and told me to turn on the TV. She said it didn't matter what channel, it's on all of them." Her voice began to waver. "Rick, she said Liz and Sean are in one of those buildings!"

"What? How does she know?"

"They were supposed to meet Sean's uncle for breakfast on the top floor of Tower 1 fifteen minutes before the first plane hit."

"A plane did that?!" Rick was incredulous.

"Two planes."

"How is that possible?—Do they think it was deliberate?—Terrorists?"

Elaine wasn't interested in theories at the moment. "Rick, my baby sister's in there! How are they supposed to get out?"

"Are they sure your sister's there? Did they try to call her cell?"

"They did, but they couldn't reach her—or Sean, either." Fear was overwhelming her, and as the tears that had been building up began to spill over, Rick sat down next to her and wrapped his arms around her.

"Why them?!" she demanded through her sobs. "She and Sean were—*are!*—such good people—" She started to say something about karma, but stopped short, knowing instinctively that Liz wouldn't appreciate the reference. Besides, she needed to be angry at someone, not at an impersonal force, so instead she blurted out, "They loved God! Why would He let this happen to them?"

Rick just stared at the screen. The disturbing images were of people hanging out windows amid the smoke, desperately waving handkerchiefs to rescue workers far below. Just then the camera caught one of them falling—or jumping. To Rick, who twenty minutes earlier had been sleeping peacefully, the sudden horror of it brought waves of nausea.

"I guess now we'll find out if He really does take care of His own," he murmured, his eyes glazing over in numb shock.

September 11, 2001, 9:20 CDT

Shannon looked around the girls' bathroom to make sure she was alone. Her heart was beating wildly, her stomach churning from the news she had just received. Her classmates were in the classroom watching the story unfold on the TV. (Some of the less mature ones just seemed glad to get out of classwork.) But no news report would tell her what she desperately needed to know.

She was not supposed to have a cell phone at school, and she usually had hers turned off, obeying the spirit, if not the letter of the law. But today was different, and she just *had* to know if they were there, or she'd go crazy!

She glanced at the door as the familiar sound of the phone's being turned on echoed off the bathroom walls. Hands trembling, she hit the speed-dial for her brother's number and listened anxiously.

The sound of numerous students' screaming came through the walls, and moments later Missy burst through the door. Her face was white, and she could barely get the words out.

"Shannon! The second Tower just collapsed!" The surreal news came at the moment

Shannon learned that her call had not gone through.

"*SEAN!*" She cried, collapsing into a heap.

CHAPTER NINETEEN

September 11, 2001, 7:00 AM EDT

Staring at the ceiling from her gilded bed, remembering nothing of the fleeting dream that had just occurred, Liz reflected on the highlights of the night before. Songs from *The Phantom of the Opera* replayed in her head as she pictured in her mind the gorgeous costumes, magnificent scenery, and breathtaking special effects. Throughout her four years in the theater department she had heard so much about *Phantom* and knew about the huge moving chandelier, the scenery rising up through the fog, and other unique aspects of the staging, but actually being there and sitting so close to the live action had been truly thrilling. It reminded her of some of the reasons she had fallen in love with the theater in the first place, and even now as she relived those moments, she got a chill. As if the sheer romance of the show hadn't been enough, she had been there with the love of her life, who was now her husband. She had got to leave with him and go back to their elegant room for another romantic night together. And unlike the show's ending, marred by heartache and guilt, they were having a glorious honeymoon, free from pain.

So far.

Suddenly realizing that this was the morning they were to meet Sean's Uncle Phil, she hurriedly got out of bed and hopped into the shower in order to be out by the time Sean got back from his run. While showering, she pondered what she should wear to meet such an important person in her husband's life. Although Sean had assured her that Uncle Phil would love her and that he had already given his uncle a rave review, for that very reason she wanted to make sure she made a good first impression. Sean had said that Windows on the World required men to wear jackets, but was there a dress code for women? "Pretty" was OK, but knowing Uncle Phil worked in the World Trade Center, she somehow felt that she should look at least a little businesslike. She finally decided to wear her grey dress pants and a pale pink shirt with a button-down collar, carrying a blazer in case someone was overzealous with the air conditioning. She toyed with the idea of making a corsage from the orchid in the bathroom but didn't know if that would scream "newlywed!" too much. She would ask Sean's opinion when he got back. *Which should be soon …* she thought as she towel-dried her hair. It was then that she caught a glimpse of the clock in the mirror. She turned to look at it directly to make sure she hadn't misread it.

He should've been back by now … Knowing Sean, he probably stopped to help an old lady across the street. Or got distracted by a fun-loving dog in the park …

8:00 AM EDT

OK, we are officially late. Liz, who had been ready for half an hour sighed with frustration; Sean had still not returned, and she didn't know whether to be furious with him or worried. How fast could he jump in the shower and throw on some clothes? She didn't know what the lines would be like at the subway station, or how long the elevators took at the World Trade Center; after all, they were going to the very top. If they were late getting to Windows on the World, would they lose their reservation? Liz tried to busy her mind with thoughts of such details, but an uneasy feeling was working its way through her consciousness in spite of her attempts to dismiss it. Sean had told her not to worry …

She had already called her mother, and she had taken the liberty of ordering coffee and finished it off. Pacing was getting old, but she had to do something with her nervous energy, made worse by the added caffeine. Finally she gave in to the urge to call him. Some would call it nagging, but what else was she supposed to do? It was less than half an hour before they were supposed to be at the other end of Manhattan, and Sean had yet to begin getting ready! She picked up her cell phone, dialed his number, and waited, staring out the window at Central Park.

Suddenly she heard a familiar little tune playing close by. There on the loveseat, where Sean had been putting on his running shoes, was his cell phone.

"Oh Sean … " she groaned, suddenly feeling utterly helpless. The feeling brought back a startling glimpse of the dream she had awakened from—the warmth of a sunny day disturbed by a sudden chill, the shadow of clouds rolling in, and sinister eyes surrounding her.

CHAPTER TWENTY

Another glorious day! Sean thought as he stretched in the morning sun. Joggers and dog walkers were already out in droves, and the early autumn air was invigorating.

He started at a quicker pace than usual, maybe because the coolness of the air and the newness of the route were energizing, or maybe because he was anxious to finish his run and get back to the luxury room and his waiting bride. He tried to focus on the pleasure of the moment, but other pleasures—recent memories and things to look forward to—flooded his thoughts until he was overwhelmed with gratitude. A silent prayer of thanks summed it up in three words: *Life is good!*

He reached the end of his run sooner than expected. *I guess time flies when you're thinking pleasant thoughts.* Perhaps thinking energy to spare was also an indication of time to spare, he decided to follow a different path for a while. He kept his eyes straight ahead so as not to trip over a small dog or collide with the elderly lady that was holding its leash or anyone else sharing the path. Occasionally he would look up and see their hotel over the tops of the trees to make sure he would have no problem getting back.

Soon he realized that his second wind was beginning to give out, and he had a stitch in his side. He stopped and looked around and was surprised at how far he had run. He turned back, holding his side and wiping the sweat from his eyes. The path seemed much longer when walking, and about ten minutes into the return trip he suddenly remembered—This was the morning that he and Liz were supposed to meet Uncle Phil at the World Trade Center for breakfast! Reaching into his pocket, he realized he had left his cell phone in the room.

"Excuse me," he asked a walker who was approaching him going the other way. "Do you have the time?" Without breaking his stride, the walker pulled out a cell phone as he passed.

"Seven fifteen," he called over his shoulder.

"Thanks," Sean called back. *Seven fifteen!?* He should have been back in the room by now. *Idiot!* he berated himself, breaking into a trot. He looked up and saw the hotel, just on the other side of the wall … He could hear the traffic, and he was pretty sure he could find a place to cut through to the front door of the hotel. Cutting sharply to his left, he ran across the grass and over some large stones.

No sooner had he crossed the boulders than he was pushed hard from behind. He staggered, trying to regain his balance, but his assailant—or perhaps a second one—tripped him, sending him slamming into the wall. Rebounding, he turned to try to catch himself. He felt, maybe even heard, a ripping in his knee. The pain didn't come for a moment, a moment in which he looked up to see who had shoved him and braced himself to face his attacker.

He saw no one.

As he wondered why anyone would shove an unarmed runner carrying no money into a wall and run away, the pain hit him like a bullet.

Collapsing to the ground, he gasped in pain then found that he was unable to exhale. The agony in his knee was only made worse by the sheer torture of trying to move it.

Lord, please. Send help!

Two women in jogging suits were walking on the path, but at such a brisk pace there didn't seem to be much chance either would look Sean's way. But just as they were about to turn, one of them glanced his way and stopped. She looked curiously at him, as her companion moved closer to her, eyeing him suspiciously as though wondering if he were hurt, faking, or merely "sleeping it off."

With a pleading look in his eyes, Sean was able to exhale enough to breathe one word: "Help!"

CHAPTER TWENTY-ONE

September 11, 2001, 8:32 AM EDT

Oh Jesus, what do I do now?

Liz sat on the edge of the bed, staring at the clock, which registered 8:32. She had even double-checked the time with Sean's cell phone and the morning news stations on TV. She had heard the same trivial news stories three times and turned it off in frustration. She felt that something was terribly wrong, but she had no idea how to find Sean. The past half hour of pacing and wondering had taken its toll, and she was an emotional wreck. Portions of her dream were coming back to her in disturbing detail—low growls, ravenous wolves closing in on her, the fur on their backs standing out, their teeth bared ...

"Lord, where *is* he?" she cried out loud.

As if in answer to her question, her cell phone rang. Shaking uncontrollably, she grabbed it.

"Sean? Where are you?!"

"Mrs. O'Brien?" a stranger's voice asked, and Liz felt as though her heart were going to beat its way out of her chest. "This is the ER at Mount Sinai Hospital. Your husband was brought here about an hour ago ... " Liz felt faint.

"What happened?! Is he going to be OK? How—?"

"He's going to be fine. He tore some ligaments running. He's being bandaged up now. However, we're going to need you to come down and bring his wallet with his ID and insurance information."

"Yes. Of course!" Liz sighed as tears of relief filled her eyes. "But I'm not familiar with New York City ... this is my first time here ... I mean, I don't know how to get to ... "

The caller understood. Apparently Sean did, too.

"Your husband said to tell you to take a cab and use the cash in his wallet."

"Oh … right … " *duh!* "that makes sense," said the flustered Liz, whose mind was still reeling. "I'm … sorry, which hospital did you say it was?"

"Mount Sinai. Have the cab bring you to the ER entrance."

"OK. Thank you so much," said Liz, slipping on her shoes. She snapped the phone shut, dropped it in her purse, grabbed Sean's wallet and a room key, and was out the door in record time.

8:48 AM, EDT

The young man with the crutches looked sheepish as his relieved bride burst through the door.

"Sean O'Brien!" she scolded. She didn't know whether to throw her arms around him and kiss him or give him the first I-told-you-so speech of his married life.

"Sorry, Hon," he said contritely, and Liz, who had become weak in the knees, sank into the chair next to his. She handed him his wallet, and he retrieved the necessary items for her to take to the receptionist.

The receptionist said she would make a copy of the information and left the window. Liz stood waiting, but even in that brief time, as the receptionist was distracted by an urgent phone call, she had to look back at her husband to reassure herself that he was all right.

"By the way, you look nice," he said.

"You mean other than the wild-eyed look of sheer terror?" said Liz, still needing to vent some residual stress. "I was so worried about you! You scared me to death!"

"Sorry, Hon," he said again. "I didn't mean to. You do look nice, though. Too bad we're missing breakfast with Uncle Phil. Did you call him by any chance?"

"Oh—! No, I didn't think of it. I was busy being relieved that you weren't lying dead somewhere in Central Park!" she said, giving him a reproachful look. "I wouldn't have known how to reach him anyway."

Sean held out his hand. "It's OK, I'll call him. I've got his number in my cell phone."

" … which is back at the hotel," said Liz. "Sorry, I didn't think of that, either. I've got mine, but there's not much battery left."

"I don't know his number off the top of my head anyway. We'll just call him as soon as we get back." After his mishap in the park, rescheduling breakfast didn't seem like a huge deal.

"OK, let's go," said Liz. She then realized that the receptionist was off the phone but was now conferring with a doctor and an aid.

"Excuse me, could I have my husband's ID and insurance card back?" she asked.

"Don't rush them," said Sean. "I'm not quite finished here, anyway." Liz noticed that he had a clipboard with numerous forms that he was only partially finished filling out.

"That's OK," said the receptionist, handing the cards back to Liz. "Just give me what you have, and you may go. We've got enough information for now."

Liz and Sean were a little surprised at the abrupt treatment and curious to see others being dismissed more promptly than Liz had ever observed in any past experience with walk-in clinics. Some doctors were talking in low tones with serious expressions, and Liz heard one say, " … need to clear this place out in the next twenty minutes."

Suddenly an aid was offering Sean a wheelchair to expedite his departure, although she didn't use those words. After helping him into the chair she began to wheel him toward the door while Liz was still gathering up his crutches, pain meds, and written instructions.

As they reached the door, the aid instructed Liz to pull up.

"I don't have a car," Liz explained. "I took a cab here. We're on our honeym—"

The aid pointed out where the cabs were and disappeared. But before Liz and Sean had time to be offended by her behavior, they noticed a steady stream of people in various hospital uniforms making their way into the building and had a feeling that this was not a typical day at Mount Sinai.

The workers looked pale and serious, and more than one glanced up at the sky to the south. Liz followed their gaze and saw smoke rising.

She vaguely recalled that the TVs in the hospital were all showing the same thing, a fire somewhere—a large building and lots of smoke. But at the time she had been too caught up in Sean's situation to think much about it. Now she thought, *That fire must be in New York!*

"Sean, what's going on?" she asked.

"I don't know," said Sean, who had been filling out forms and also missed the story. "But it doesn't look good."

Just then a taxi pulled up, and an elderly lady began to get out. Immediately a man wearing a hospital ID badge approached and spoke to her and the driver. The woman looked alarmed and got back into the cab.

"Can we share this taxi?" Liz asked before she had had a chance to shut the door. The woman looked stunned and didn't answer.

"Where you going?" the driver asked.

Liz told him, and he said, "Hop in." Liz helped Sean in, handed him the crutches, ran around to the other side, and got in next to the lady.

"What did that man say to you?" Sean asked the driver as they were pulling out.

"He said they're cancelling all non-emergency procedures today."

"The whole hospital? Why?" asked Liz.

"Probably because of the fire at the World Trade Center."

"World Trade Center?!" said Sean and Liz simultaneously.

"What happened?" asked Sean.

"Plane just crashed right into one of the Twin Towers. Bad fire. We gotta stay clear of the whole area."

"But ... we were going there this morning," said Liz.

"Not now, you ain't," said the cab driver. Liz and Sean looked at each other.

"Which tower got hit?" asked Liz.

"Tower 1, the North Tower," he told her.

Liz looked at Sean, whose ashen face confirmed her fear.

"Is that the one with the restaurant on top?" she asked anyone who was listening.

"Yes. It is," said the woman, whose face had also turned white. "My daughter works there," she added grimly.

"Uncle Phil ... " Sean's voice was somewhere between a whisper and a whimper.

"What floor does he work on?" The moment the words were out Liz questioned the wisdom of asking. Uncle Phil wouldn't have been there anyway, he'd have been waiting for them at the restaurant. Sean didn't respond, and she didn't ask again.

Liz watched intently out the window, but it was maddening to be surrounded by tall buildings and unable to see what was going on in the direction of the World Trade Center. Whenever the cab crossed an intersection the view opened up momentarily, revealing black, billowing clouds. Clusters of pedestrians were gathered at each street corner, staring at the smoke, all in wide-eyed amazement, some in sheer terror.

Soon the traffic was so congested that the passengers could have walked to the hotel faster, had Sean not been on crutches. The news reports coming over the radio seemed surreal enough, but when the news broke that a second plane had slammed into the South Tower, suspicions were confirmed that this had been a deliberate attack.

The driver ceased his comments, the lady buried her face in her hands, and Liz felt faint. Sean was the one who verbalized what everyone was thinking.

"So we're at war," he said, staring blankly out the window.

After what seemed like hours in the cab, Liz and Sean paid the driver and hurried into the hotel, where people were gathered around the TVs in various sitting areas. The screens showed images of people standing in the windows of the Twin Towers, desperately waving handkerchiefs to the rescuers below. The brightness of the sunlight shining onto the building gave the scene a weird irony.

Suddenly Liz heard numerous people gasp in unison and wondered if she had really seen what she thought she had seen.

"Sean, did someone just jump?" she cried gripping his arm. She was feeling sick.

"Let's go upstairs," Sean said decisively, hobbling toward the elevator. Liz followed, glad to get away from the crowds.

Once in the room, Sean found his cell phone and hastily found Uncle Phil's number. Liz watched his face as he waited, and knew immediately that he had not reached his uncle.

"Cell phone use is down," he announced with disgust and frustration, sinking into the loveseat and tossing the useless device onto the bed.

Liz sat down beside him. "We need to pray," she said, trying to take his hands, but Sean was busy with the remote, staring at the same series of disturbing pictures they had seen downstairs. They knew by now that there were some people who could not get out of the building, and Liz had a sinking feeling that if these people couldn't get out, what chance did those on the top floors have? She didn't dare ask any more questions about Uncle Phil, so all she could do was sit beside Sean and pray silently, though she hardly knew how to pray. For a brief moment she would sense the presence of God, the next moment the horrific events of the morning would seem to take on a life of their own, terrorizing her and making her acutely aware of her helplessness and mortality.

Although she had a hard time praying, there was no limit to the number of things she could worry about. She worried about her parents and the fact that she couldn't contact them. She worried about Nana's emotional state. Could the stress of such an event cause her to have another heart attack? She worried about the people in the buildings who couldn't get out, and she worried about their families.

And of course, she worried about Uncle Phil.

And then it occurred to her: if she could worry about it, she could pray about it.

She forced herself to focus her thoughts on God and asking Him for help.

But as if to stop her prayers in her tracks, the next thing she saw was the mind-numbing picture of one of the towers collapsing. It was a nightmare in slow motion, enveloped in a charcoal-colored cloud. The thought of all the people who were still inside was unfathomable, and Liz became aware that Sean was slumped over, his head in his hands, his shoulders quivering as he tried in vain to suppress a sob.

Liz heard the reporter announce in a shaking voice that the South Tower was collapsing; oddly, the first tower hit was still standing. She had no idea what the chances were that the people in the North Tower could still be rescued, but she tried to encourage her husband anyway.

"Sean, that was the South Tower, it's not the one Uncle Phil is in! We can still pray that they'll get the fire put out … that … that they'll send helicopters to rescue the people at the top, or … " Her voice trailed off. Sean's shoulders were heaving, and Liz rubbed his back, feeling that sense of helplessness again, utterly at a loss for words.

Suddenly she remembered something Sean had told her when she was worried and grief-stricken over the state of their beloved choir director. The gifted man had been hit by a drunk driver and had sustained life-threatening brain injuries. When severe seizures had struck in the middle of a rehearsal, Liz's perspective had been stuck in temporal mode, focusing not on the eternal God but on the present exhibit of human frailty.

She remembered the sight of her dear mentor being whisked away in an ambulance, how her thoughts had been a tangled assortment of doubts, questions, and fears that she would never see him again. Just as the darkness was closing in on her soul, Sean had reminded her that they would see him again—if not in this life, in a brighter, happier life that would go on forever. It hadn't made everything instantly OK, but she had felt the darkness lift a little as she set her mind on the Bigger Picture. Sean's words had helped her then. Maybe the same words coming from her would help him now.

"He's going to be OK. We know that, don't we?" Sean's swollen eyes looked up at her. "Either way, he'll be OK," Liz went on, trying to smile into those despairing eyes. "That's what you told me about Mr. Walker, remember?" Liz's voice was shaky, but in spite of the enormity of the situation she was beginning to take an eternal perspective. She watched his face to catch a glimmer of light. "The same is true for Uncle Phil, right? I may not meet him today, but someday I will … right?"

Sean just stared at her, and again she had that sinking feeling.

"But there's one big difference between him and Mr. Walker, Liz," he said in a choked voice. He then said the words Liz dreaded: "Uncle Phil doesn't know Jesus."

And as Sean again buried his face in his hands, the nightmare was back, and darkness closed in once more.

CHAPTER TWENTY-TWO

September 12, 2001, 9:00 AM EDT

It was a small picture—tiny, actually—and not a very clear one, but it was all Sean had. The thought of that miniscule snapshot among the sea of faces of missing loved ones only intensified the feelings of hopelessness.

"But we have to try," said Liz, desperately wanting to ease her beloved's pain. "Hey, if God wants someone to see it, they will, won't they?" Apparently Sean didn't share her optimism.

"I don't even know how much it still looks like him," Sean moaned, his head in his hands. Liz looked more closely at the picture that had been in Sean's wallet for the past five years. It was like looking at a younger version of Sean's father, or of Sean's twin brother. The twenty-something man had the O'Brien eyes and smile she had come to love, warm, friendly, the kind expression that said, "I like you. You're OK."

"Is he as encouraging as you are?" she asked.

"Well, he wasn't always," Sean replied with the hint of a smirk. "He was only a few years older than me. My parents were actually already engaged by the time he was born. He was my grandparents' little 'surprise package.'" Liz smiled. "Yeah, when my parents got married my Uncle Steven was a groomsman, but Uncle Phil couldn't even be a ring bearer, he was just a baby.

"When I was little he would tease me something awful at every family get-together. He was a real pro at it, knew exactly when he could get away with it. I'd get so mad, then when I was starting to swing at him and trying to kick him or bite him, one of the grownups would show up, and suddenly he'd be all angelic. Of course, I'd get reprimanded and told to behave myself, and he'd get praised for his patience and maturity."

"And this is your favorite uncle?" Liz teased.

"Well, people change. My parents moved to Texas for a time, and when we came back to Chicago I was a freshman in high school. I was already stressing out about being a freshman and being in a new school, but when I heard Uncle Phil was a senior in the same school, I really dreaded that first day."

"So ... how was it?" Liz asked, relieved that Sean was talking, which was much better than fretting or brooding.

"It wasn't long before I got accosted by a couple of juniors. I was trying to open my locker, and one of them kept twirling the dial just as I was done with the combination. Soon they were both laughing at me, saying stuff about the way my ears stuck out."

"Your ears?"

"Yeah. Mom tried a home haircut on me that left me pretty much bald, but that's another sad story for another day ... Anyway, I was just trying not to cry or do anything else that would make things worse than they already were.

"Then Uncle Phil showed up, and I thought, 'Great. Here he comes to finish me off.' But instead he said something like 'Hey, whatcha doin' with my nephew?' He was grinning when he said it, and I still didn't know what to expect, but those two seemed surprised to learn we were related. They turned to him, and the way they looked at him told me they had a lot of respect for him. They were smiling, but they looked nervous." Sean smiled at the memory, and Liz got the feeling this story had a happy ending.

"So he came to your defense?"

"Well ... sort of. Actually, he just kind of deflected the humor onto himself. He said something like, 'you didn't recognize the famous O'Brien ears?' and pulled his hair back—I think he was pushing his own ears a little to make them stick out even more than mine. Then he let go a bunch of big-ear jokes that got us all laughing—me laughing with relief!—and basically said when it came to big ears, I was an amateur, and if they wanted to see a pro, he was it. The bell rang, and the juniors went off to class—still laughing. I had no idea where my first class was, so Phil walked me there. And on the way he gave me some advice." Sean's eyes teared up as he remembered the words that reflected his uncle's philosophy of life.

"He said, 'When people try to embarrass you by laughing at you, just laugh with 'em. It takes all the wind outa their sails, and you just might end up with a new friend.' He was kinda my hero after that day."

"Did he always come to your rescue?"

"I'm not sure he ever had to again. Word got around that I was his nephew. That and knowing he was never far off gave me confidence, and that may have been all I needed to get me through that first year."

Liz thought for a moment about what Sean had been saying, then said, "What a neat guy … Are you sure he's not a Christian?" The moment she'd said it, she kicked herself for bringing up the "bad news" part of the situation.

Sean thought about it, and for a moment it seemed he was trying to convince himself otherwise, but finally he said, sighing, "Well, he wasn't the last time I saw him. He was doing great on his own, thank you very much, and it was hard for anyone to argue with that. He was successful, content, and people love him. What's not to love? Come to think of it, he told me on one occasion that if he ever 'got religion' as he called it, I'd be the first to know."

There was a long pause, as Sean continued to brood and Liz tried desperately and unsuccessfully to think of something she could say to make it all better. Flashes of the dream she had had the day before still haunted her, but she had the feeling there had been more to it than the desperate situation she was remembering—the darkness, the cold, the wolves …

Then Sean's voice broke as he cried, "Liz, he's got to be alive! I can't stand the thought of … " He couldn't finish the sentence, and all Liz could do was wrap her arms around him and say a silent prayer.

CHAPTER TWENTY-THREE

September 11, 2001, 7:58 AM EDT

"'Morning, Phil ... Late night?" Phil snapped out of his daze at hearing the familiar voice among the many in the lobby of the North Tower.

"Oh, hi, Ben ... No, I just got back from Tokyo Sunday." Phil yawned.

"A little jet lag?"

"That's as good an excuse as any."

Ben looked at his watch. "7:58. So what time is it in Tokyo?"

"If you're expecting me to do the math at this hour of the morning, ... " Phil laughed.

"Well let me buy you breakfast, anyway" Ben offered. The doors opened, and the two joined the flow of passengers boarding the Skylobby Express.

"Thanks," said Phil, "but I'll have to take a rain check. My nephew and his new bride are here for a visit. We're meeting for breakfast, and I'll be showing them around."

"Your nephew just got married?"

"Yeah, Saturday. I hated to miss it, but the wedding was in Michigan anyway."

Ben had a strange expression on his face as he muttered "small world ... " Then, changing the subject, he asked, "Are we still meeting this afternoon to go over the Kraft account?"

"Sure. I'll be back to business by then. I'll have Saundra get the papers together this morning."

"Sure, let Saundra do it," Ben kidded. "You sure have a knack for getting other people to do your work for you."

"Hey, it's a gift," Phil explained with mock humility.

The two continued ribbing each other as the elevator made its way to the 43rd floor. Phil and Ben got off with the others and headed for the "local" elevators to take them the rest of the way to the 88th floor.

"See you this afternoon, Phil," said Ben when they had arrived at their destination. "And try to wake up by then."

"Will do, Ben."

Once in his office, Phil took a moment to take in the Manhattan skyline. The early morning sunlight that reflected off the surrounding buildings was dazzling, giving him a surge of self-satisfaction in getting as far as he had.

"Good morning, Mr. O'Brien," an attractive young woman greeted him, holding two mugs of coffee. "Cream, no sugar," she smiled, handing one to him.

"Thanks, Saundra." Phil took the coffee and seated himself in the swiveling armchair between his desk and the Manhattan view. *Life is good,* he thought.

"Oh, Saundra," he stopped her as she reached the door. "I'm going up to Windows on the World to have breakfast with my nephew and his wife at 8:30. Would you get the papers for the Kraft account together for my meeting this afternoon with Ben Jacobson?"

"I'll have them on your desk right away," Saundra responded agreeably.

Beautiful and efficient, Phil congratulated himself. He was glad Saundra wasn't one of those NOW-type women. As bright as she was, she had no problem making the coffee in the morning and bringing everyone a cup; in fact, she seemed to enjoy doing it. She also had no problem with having the door held open for her. The atmosphere of the office was enhanced by her philosophy that there was nothing condescending or undignified about people's being nice to one another. Phil had more than once invited her to call him by his first name, but she seemed more comfortable calling him "Mr. O'Brien." *A little old-fashioned, but that's OK,* he thought.

Phil sat sipping his coffee and looking out at the Manhattan skyline shining in the morning sun. A tiny object on the side of one of the buildings caught his eye. He opened his desk drawer, took out a pair of high-powered binoculars, and stepped over to the window.

To his astonishment, a lone window washer was perched dozens of floors above the street, running his squeegee across the windows with energy that was admirable at that hour of the morning. The man looked young by his build, was dressed in white, and wore a safari hat to block some of the glare of the morning rays.

Man, I didn't even know windows got dirty that far off the ground, Phil thought, grateful that he didn't have that kind of job. The thought of spending his life washing other people's windows and getting paid what he considered a pittance was not a pleasant one, but it made Phil stop and consider that for all he knew, if things had been just a little different, if *he* had been a little different, he just might have ended up in a job like that one.

As he breathed in the aroma of the coffee and watched the window washer, almost mesmerized by the back-and-forth strokes of the squeegee, he found himself reflecting on the events of his life that had brought him to the enviable position he was in.

Phil had known early on that he had a quick wit; by the end of grade school he had already mastered the clever comeback. One of his favorite teachers had observed his tendency to poke fun at others, making some cry and others laugh and join in the mocking. Instead of chewing him out for tormenting his peers, she had told him privately that he had a God-given gift of a keen sense of humor, which would get him far, *if* he used it wisely. She had admonished him to make fun of himself instead of others, thus building bridges and tearing down walls, instead of the other way around.

After getting into trouble a few more times for crushing another student with his words, Phil had decided to follow the teacher's advice, and soon found himself to be the most popular kid in school. In a very short time he had gone from being class bully to life of the party.

Years later, a business professor had explained the importance of showing an interest in others, and Phil had quickly cultivated the habit of acting interested in people, whether or not he truly was. He had become proficient at asking questions that showed interest and at the same time reading an individual to discern the boundaries as to how personal those questions should be. Over time he had effectively turned "interest in others" into an art form.

Eventually, by fine-tuning his people skills, Phil had become not only a success in the business world, but also the most beloved member of the sales team. And here he was, Vice President in charge of Sales, doing what he did best and watching the company's sales skyrocket—in the World Trade Center, no less. Sean would be impressed. In fact, Phil mused, with his acting skills, Sean just might be inspired to pursue the same career path, once he saw how far salesmanship could get him.

Sure beats washing windows, he thought, lifting the binoculars to his eyes for one more look at the high-wire act. The worker was finishing up a section of windows, and just as Phil was focusing the lenses on him, the man turned, smiled, and gave him a friendly wave.

What the—? thought Phil, nearly dropping the binoculars. How could that man have seen him from so far away? He didn't have time to ponder the question, as just then Saundra appeared at the door.

"Excuse me, Mr. O'Brien?" she said, interrupting his train of thought. "Weren't you going to meet your nephew at 8:30?" Phil glanced at his watch and was surprised to find that it was already 8:47.

"Oh, for—!" he chastised himself, jumping up and grabbing his jacket.

Just then he heard a loud roar close by, and before he had time to wonder what it was, a heavy boom rocked the building. As long as he had worked in the North Tower, Phil had never felt it rock like this before.

A bomb! was his immediate thought, remembering the explosions in the parking garage that had killed six people and injured a thousand in '93. This had sounded much closer than the parking garage, and the giant fireball he saw from his window confirmed that this was very close, very big, or both.

"What was that!?" cried Saundra.

"I'm not sure. Are you OK?"

"What do we do?" she cried, giving way to panic. It was then that Phil noticed the room was filling with smoke and everything in the office was getting drenched.

Oh great, he thought. *There goes the sprinkler system.* He then realized that the water wasn't coming from the sprinklers but from burst pipes overhead. *OK, that's way too close.* He muttered an expletive, grabbed his briefcase, and took a quick check around to make sure all the file cabinets were closed. Then seeing the increasing smoke and flames outside, he decided it would be best to deal with the mess later. Right now he had a near-hysterical office assistant to try to placate.

"We'd better get out of here until someone can determine the extent of the damage," he said, trying to sound calm and businesslike.

Even without instructions, common sense told them not to take the elevator. All over the office people were looking questioningly at one another. The younger ones seemed to be wondering if they should get back to work. Phil knew better, however, and headed for the stairwell, followed by his dutiful office assistant. He spotted Ben, and the two exchanged glances as if to say, *Well, this is a great way to start the day.* They reached the stairwell at the same time, both dripping wet, and Ben said, "Well, Phil, I hope those papers are in a waterproof pouch!"

Phil instinctively motioned to Saundra to go first, and she didn't hesitate to comply. She grabbed the handrail just in time to steady herself as her foot slipped on the wet stairs.

"I hope the express is still running," Phil thought out loud as they neared the Sky-lobby. The thought of walking down another 43 floors was daunting.

But when they reached the lobby any thought of taking the easy way down dissolved as they quickly learned that these elevators were not running, either. (The word "fireball" could be heard in the excited chatter.) They heard the massive steel of the building, which had been known to sway slightly in a strong wind, now groaning and making hideous clanking sounds, and it was evident that the structure was leaning. Saudra gasped.

"It's falling over! We're going to die!" she whimpered.

"Maybe so," Phil stated, "but we'll die running!" He grabbed her hand and pulled her toward the stairwell, followed by Ben. The narrow space made one claustrophobic, and the thought of all those flames added to the urgency of the situation. Another sobering thought was just how many flights of stairs remained between them and the street. It must have occurred to all three of them at the same time, as they had stopped talking; in fact, no one was saying anything, just watching the growing stream of people ahead of them. The stairwell was becoming more and more congested, and all they could do was to keep moving at a snail's pace, staring at the backs of the people in front of them, silently willing them to go faster.

A few more floors down, Phil thought of Sean and Liz. Had they been waiting for him at the restaurant, above the crash? And if so, how in the world were they going to get out? He tried to shut out the image of the flaming debris from his mind; the thought was too disturbing, and out of his control anyway.

Although it seemed like an eternity, it had only been about fifteen minutes since the original crash when another muffled explosion was felt. A collective gasp echoed up and down the stairwell. Minutes later a pager went off, and soon, amid murmurs of incredulity, word spread that planes had hit both towers.

Then it wasn't an accident, Phil thought as a sick feeling came over him.

We're under attack, Ben thought grimly.

CHAPTER TWENTY-FOUR

By the time they reached the twentieth floor, the downward flow of people was becoming intolerably slow, since everyone from the lower floors had been trying to enter the stairwell all at the same time; there was no such thing as an express stairwell. Water was now pouring down the stairs, and people were helping one another along. Two men supported someone on crutches and another carried a woman who was unable to make it alone. The reality of their peril was sinking in, and Phil began to wonder seriously whether they were going to get out alive.

You could've worked in a small office building in Chicago, he chided himself, *but oh no, you had to be a big shot and work on the 88th floor of the World Trade Center!*

The downward climb was taking on a surreal quality. Phil could hear Saundra crying as they made their way down at an agonizingly slow pace. He wanted to comfort her, but although he was rarely at a loss for words, he found himself speechless. He was bothered by her weeping and thinking that there were moments—like this one—when a tough NOW-type would be more convenient. His usually jovial demeanor was gone. The sense of helplessness was making him irritable. He was used to being in control at all times, and he fought off the unwelcome thought that there was absolutely nothing he could do about the present situation.

What seemed like years later, the line had come to a complete stand-still. Word was being passed up ordering everyone to line up single file.

Single file!? Why the—?! Phil wanted to put an end to this nonsense and just get out of there. He might have begun bellowing orders for everyone to move it, but he was stifled by a growing sense of terror. Everyone else appeared to be handling the situation with the utmost politeness and consideration. Was he the only one that understood the need to get out *now*? Then he saw the reason everyone was pressed against the wall; on the other side of the stairs people were coming *up*. Firefighters, loaded down with heavy gear were actually heading *toward* what everyone else was fleeing *from*. The sight of them was devastating. Their faces resembled those of soldiers going to battle—somber, fearful, yet determined, the epitome of courage.

Some of these guys aren't going to make it out alive, Phil thought, overcome by a feeling that was completely alien to him, a humbling blend of shame, admiration, pity, and gratitude. Any other thoughts of taking charge or complaining dissolved with every stoic face that passed. He saw someone ahead of him offer a fireman a bottle of water and wished he had something to give them, something expressing his utmost respect.

It took another forty minutes to reach the ground floor, but the refugees were to find out that they weren't in the clear yet. The floor was strewn with glass from shattered windows, and teams of firefighters were everywhere, waiting their turn to go up into the blazing tower. Outside fireballs of flaming debris were showering down on the courtyard, dismissing any notion of exiting the building that way any time soon. Oddly, although the power had been knocked out virtually everywhere else, the escalators to the lower level were still running, and the fleeing people were directed to take them down to the mall.

It all seemed to Phil like a bad dream. What hours earlier had been a shining, spacious lobby, decked with dozens of colorful flags from every nation, was now a disaster area. Stunned survivors who had been descending stairs for nearly an hour now stepped onto the escalators and stood staring into the gloom as they were being carried below street level. Some seemed to be in shock, others seemed to be acting almost normally, running "on automatic," as though the magnitude of the situation had yet to catch up with them; perhaps they were simply in denial.

At the bottom of the escalators water was everywhere. Over the noise of the crowd and the water, firefighters' voices could be heard shouting directions and trying to keep everyone moving. Phil and Ben made their way to an escalator going up to the street.

As the crowds emerged, many of them paused, oblivious to the fact that thousands of people behind them also wanted to get out. Firefighters reminded them loudly and repeatedly to keep moving.

"Let's go up to Fulton Street," Ben suggested. The dazed men followed the flow of people walking north, away from the inferno.

No sooner had they started out than they heard a sound like thunder, which quickly grew to the magnitude of dozens of freight trains. The last human sounds they heard before the roar drowned out everything else were voices shrieking. "Oh God! It's collapsing!" Phil glanced back to see the South Tower begin to crumble, imploding in a surreal, slow-motion nightmare. For a moment he froze in disbelief.

As if the shock of that sight weren't enough, the people on the street quickly became aware that a gigantic, billowing black cloud was fast approaching, threatening to bury them all alive. Phil and Ben instinctively ducked around a corner in time to see a black tidal wave thundering down the street. Although out of the main path of the debris, the two men could not escape the billows of ash that spread and soon had enveloped everything and everyone in darkness. Suddenly there was an eerie silence as the dark cloud muffled out the noise that moments before had been overwhelming. The men grabbed their shirts and held them up to their faces in a feeble attempt to breathe clean air.

The voice was loud, clear, and close. Where it had come from was a mystery, but it was a woman's voice Phil had never heard before.

"You boys come with me!" it ordered. Somehow Phil and Ben knew the woman was speaking to them, and she spoke with such authority that, having no other options in mind, they instinctively began to follow as closely as they could, lest the voice get swallowed up in the dark silence, leaving them behind. But where was she taking them? They were so disoriented in the darkness that they weren't even sure what street they were on. They staggered dumbly peering into the dark grey until they heard the same voice sternly order, "THIS WAY! Go to the church!"

Phil felt a woman's hand firmly grab his and yank him along with more strength than he could imagine a woman's having.

"Ben?!" he heard his own muffled voice cry out.

"Right behind you!" came the muffled reply as Ben grabbed Phil's belt.

A fleeting thought ran through both their minds,—other than who was this woman, and why was she helping them?—and that was, *How do we know the church won't be next?* But what choice was there? They were clinging irrationally to the authority they heard in the woman's voice, trying to ignore the fact that she spoke with a distinctly Southern accent and that there was a definite possibility she knew absolutely nothing about New York City.

Meanwhile it was becoming harder and harder to breathe, and any other thoughts were soon taken over by one desperate need: AIR! Whether it was worse to inhale the soot through their shirts or to try to make it to the church without breathing at all, both men were sure they were going to die—they and a thousand others who had made it out of the towering fireball only to be buried in the ashes below.

They reached the church sooner than expected. It was a good thing, because their lungs were burning and crying out for air in violent spasms. The moment they burst through the door of the church they began gasping and coughing uncontrollably. The lady slammed the door tightly behind them to shut out the avalanche as quickly as possible. Soon a strong hand was slapping them on the back, and the motherly voice was saying with reassuring authority, "Easy now, you'll be OK." As their eyes adjusted to the light, for the first time they got a look at their savior. She was an unlikely heroine, plump, middle-aged, and in spite of being covered with ash, she had a certain joy in her eyes that defied the situation. Phil found it surprising (and a little annoying) that this motherly woman seemed scarcely out of breath, and here they were, the young males, gasping for air.

"That was quite a run, wasn't it?" she declared. "Y'all come in here and rest." As she led them into the sanctuary there were other things that surprised them, such as the light that filled the sanctuary.

"I thought the power would be out all over Manhattan. Does the church have a generator?" Ben asked the lady, who seemed familiar with the place. She smiled confidently.

"My boss never loses power," she said.

Her confidence seemed a little naïve to Phil, especially when the realization hit him that this couldn't be Trinity Church. They hadn't run far enough, and this place certainly wasn't big enough. Having attended a wedding or two at Trinity Church he was familiar with the extravagant, ornate style of that sanctuary. This church, though beautiful, was decidedly simpler in its décor. As he looked around at his surroundings he had a sinking feeling. This was the historic church, just a few yards from the World Trade Center! It was hundreds of years old; in fact, he had heard something about George Washington's having worshiped there. If the South Tower, with its steel girders and modern engineering had crumbled, what chance did this tiny church have? Especially if the nearby North Tower collapsed as well; they would be buried alive.

The eerie silence outside was the opposite of what one might expect when airplanes were crashing and buildings burning and crumbling. *If this is a dream, it's the longest one I've ever had,* Phil thought. In contrast to the brightness of the day's beginning and the dark horror of the agonizing minutes that had followed, the pastel walls gave the sanctuary an other-worldly mood.

Phil was trying to get a grip on reality, and while the Southern lady seemed an unlikely person to consult, she had been the one who had brought them to safety—temporarily at least—and obviously knew her way around. She had picked up a mop and was cleaning up the soot where they had come in.

"The South Tower's gone, isn't it?" he asked her. It was more a statement than a question; the reality of it was still just beginning to sink in.

The woman stopped mopping and looked at him somberly. "Honey, both towers are gone." Her words hit him like a freight train. "And there'll be more buildings gone before the day's over."—Another freight train! As she went back to mopping, she continued.

"The Pentagon's a mess … " *The Pentagon! But that's in—!* "and another plane crashed in New Jersey. Some brave people on that flight … " Feeling sick, not even questioning how she knew, Phil sank into the pew next to Ben.

"It's not the buildings that're the important things. You know that, don't you?" the lady said. She didn't wait for either of them to respond. "It's the people. A lot of people left this world today. Lot o' people went to be with Jesus … " She stopped mopping. " … and a lot didn't." She sighed sadly. "Trouble is, a lot o' people don't even think about eternity 'til it's too late. Not one of those people thought this would be their last day on earth."

"The thought sure didn't occur to me," Phil muttered. He looked around at the hundreds of panes of glass. "Shouldn't we be in the basement or something?—Away from breaking glass, I mean?" he asked. *Not that it matters that much,* he thought. *It'd probably just postpone the inevitable.* With the World Trade Center crumbling all around them, it was just a matter of time before …

"Naw, you boys just set here and rest," the lady assured them. "You'll be fahn." She went to put the mop away, leaving Phil and Ben to sort through what she had said … the buildings … the people … eternity … it was too much for Phil.

Had the situation been on a smaller scale, this would have been the kind of moment where Phil would say something clever and light to put everyone at ease, but this experience was so out of his league that he had long come to the end of himself. Whatever strength he'd had of his own had dissolved somewhere between the foyer and the sanctuary. Utterly overwhelmed, he collapsed into a helpless heap. Soon he felt a warm arm around him; it was Ben's.

As long as the two of them had known each other, they had never had any physical contact except for the compulsory handshake. The simple gesture of kindness at such a moment was so unexpected that a sudden flood of emotions overtook Phil. For the first time in many years, he began to sob, as Ben patted his back awkwardly. A couple of hours ago Phil had been on top of the world, a cocky young executive, anticipating impressing his nephew with—

"SEAN!" Phil's head snapped up. "Ben! My nephew was coming to see me with his new wife!" Ben looked at him questioningly. "They were meeting me at Windows on the World at 8:30!" He racked his brain, trying to remember the events of the last hours. Then with a sinking feeling, he remembered.

"I was running late—it was after 8:30 when the plane hit!" Phil felt sick to his stomach.

"If they were already there … !"

Ben's heart went out to his friend. "Got your cell phone?" he asked.

"Of course!" In his panic, Phil hadn't been thinking clearly. With fumbling hands, he took his cell phone from his pocket, found Sean's number, and pressed "send."

For several seconds Phil stared at the phone in bewilderment.

"I can't get through. Oh God … " he whimpered. Ben tried to reassure him.

"Now we don't know for sure if they were in the building," he pointed out.

Phil's face was the picture of misery.

For a long time neither Phil nor Ben said a word. Unrelated thoughts raced through their minds, events of their lives replayed in random order. Maybe it was something about the sounds of the familiar hymns the lady was humming in the other room that made them focus their thoughts on the eternal and infinite. Though neither spoke, they both began looking for some overarching theme that would somehow make sense of it all and give meaning to everything. Finally Ben broke the agonizing silence.

"So, your nephew got married … Saturday, did you say?"

"Yeah … Saturday … " Phil confirmed absently.

"My … " Ben seemed hesitant to bring up the subject. "My sister was married Saturday, too."

At first Phil wanted to snap, "What does that have to do with anything?" but in their present situation making small talk was better than sitting in the dim light, driving themselves crazy with questions that had no answers.

"I didn't know you had a sister," he said. *Does it take something like this to really get to know a person?*

"According to my parents, I don't."

Phil's mind was still on Sean and Liz, but realizing that obsessing over them was no help, he forced himself to focus on what Ben was saying. Maybe this wasn't small talk after all. He noticed Ben seemed pensive, and Phil thought he might have brought up the subject for a reason.

"I'm sorry ... What did you say about your parents?"

"They sort of disowned my sister. As far as they're concerned, she's dead." The moment Ben said it, he cringed. *Not a good word to use at a time like this.*

"Why on earth ... ?" Phil asked, incredulous. After what had transpired in the past couple of hours, he couldn't imagine what sort of family squabble would make anyone want to count a living child as dead.

"They ... we considered her a traitor," Ben said softly, not at all proud of what he was saying.

"Because ... ?" Phil spoke partly because he had become genuinely curious, partly because he could sense that Ben wanted to talk about it, and he too wanted to keep the dialog going rather than sit in the sanctuary with its blackened windows and eerie silence outside.

"She denied the faith my parents had built their whole lives upon, and that was considered unforgivable."

"How did she deny the faith?" Phil wondered. He had never seen any sign of religious devotion in Ben before, and the subject of personal beliefs had never come up. But at the moment the idea of some kind of belief system was suddenly, surprisingly relevant.

"Mom and Dad were—are—Orthodox Jews. And I guess I'm supposed to be, too," he added parenthetically. "They do everything according to tradition—you know, eat a kosher diet, keep the Sabbath and all that. When I'm home I do it, too, but it's never been as important to me as it is to them, just something I've always gone along with to keep the peace. I guess Rebecca was the same way, but then she found something else that was more real to her, and my parents took it like she'd stabbed them in the back."

"Real," Phil mused. "What is real?" Their situation still seemed dreamlike, but he was beginning to realize that he was not going to wake up from it, and the problems were not going to be resolved any time soon. There was a sense of darkness closing in—not just the ash that blocked out the sun, but an evil presence without that was almost palpable. Phil kept talking to Ben, trying to keep it at bay. "What was it your sister found?"

"Well, I guess it was more of a 'who.' Becca started to believe that Yeshua—Jesus—was God. We'd always respected him as a rabbi and historical figure, but to put him on the same level as Jehovah was ... just wrong."

"Do you know where she is now?"

"Somewhere in Michigan. The church she got married in was in a little town called Onaway." Ben had a look of profound sadness. "She sent an invitation to the family, but it was thrown out with the junk mail."

"But you read it first," Phil deduced.

"Yeah, I read it," Ben confessed. "I fished it out of the trash and hung onto it, actually, and ... " There was a long pause, during which the deadly quiet brought back the awareness of the Dark Presence outside.

Keep talking, Phil!

"You hung onto it because ... ?"

Ben hesitated, then admitted, "I decided to go. Without telling the rest of the family, of course. Fortunately I'd done business in Detroit on several occasions, so I could fly there without raising a lot of questions."

"What did she say when she saw you?" asked Phil, who was becoming interested in spite of himself.

Ben almost smiled in amusement as he shook his head.

"She didn't see me. I'd planned to just slip in and sit in the back, but when I saw how small the church was, I just waited across the street in my rental car."

"You mean after all that you didn't go to the wedding?"

"Well," Ben began, his face turning red, "I waited 'til I saw them close the doors. Then I walked over and listened under an open window. Yeah, I know it's crazy. Not very dignified or businesslike. But I still love my sister, whatever she's done."

CHAPTER TWENTY-FOUR

September 11, 2001, evening

How much time had passed, the two young executives had no clue. Having temporarily run out of things to say to distract them from their predicament, they sat in their pew, staring at the cross at the front of the sanctuary. Beyond the dozens of windowpanes they could see nothing but the grey darkness; inside the sanctuary glowed with the soft light that seemed to come from nowhere and everywhere at the same time. Phil and Ben could hear the voice of the Southern woman still humming old hymns in another part of the church. Finally Ben returned to their conversation.

"He gave her roses," he said.

Phil was uncertain to whom his friend was referring, but then he remembered they had been talking about Ben's sister's wedding.

"Roses!" Ben repeated as if to say, *Can you believe it?*

"That's a nice gesture, romantic. Groom sounds like a nice guy."

"Not the groom. Yeshua. He gave Becca roses. Hundreds of them. I could even smell them."

"You say Yeshua—Jesus—gave them to her? How do you figure that?"

"There's no way she and that groom of hers could have paid for that many roses, and even if they could, they're too smart to spend that much money on such a thing, not in their situation."

"But they had friends, didn't they? ... Why would you think that ... He ... "

"I heard the preacher tell the people about it. A big truck just dropped them off, said there's been some kind of mistake, and they could have 'em free of charge."

"You're kidding! So they figured it was Yesh ... Him?"

"You got a better explanation?"

"That's pretty amazing."

"That was my thought. The guests all gasped, then laughed, then applauded, like it was one big inside joke. There was even something special about the fact that they were red roses.

"When the service was over I hurried back to the car and watched from across the street. When they flung the doors open, I could see them—big red roses all over the church. (I could've sworn I smelled them, even from across the street.) Becca had a huge bouquet of them, her bridesmaids each had a bouquet, and the groomsmen each had one in his lapel."

The two men sat pensively staring at the Cross at the front of the church. Finally Phil broke the silence.

"Well, I don't care about roses, but I sure hope J.C. will get us out of this mess." For a moment Phil felt guilty for being so presumptuous. Why would He care about them—two guys with their fox-hole faith—with all the other people, good people that were in danger that day? Good people like Saundra—what had happened to her?

Ben hesitated as the thought occurred to him.

"He seems to have taken care of us so far." The men exchanged glances and went back to staring at the Cross in awed silence.

Although the world outside had been dark all day, Phil's watch now told him that true night was falling. His friend had finally succumbed to the weariness that comes from extreme stress, followed by a sprint, followed by a long heart-to-heart talk. Ben was sleeping soundly on the pew in the back, and Phil had moved toward the front, though not knowing exactly why.

His mind was still reeling with the thought of his own helplessness, a thought still so foreign to him. He had never been helpless before in his life.

Well, that wasn't quite true. Of course he had been completely dependent as a baby, before he could even make his needs known clearly. But he didn't remember those days. His first memories were of being a child in preschool. ... Of course he had been dependent there, too. He had felt like a big boy because he could walk, but he had unknowingly depended upon his parents to see that he didn't walk into the street or the swimming pool. He had felt independent, but of course he wasn't really. Then he had become a cocky, popular teenager ... Well, he had been dependent then, too, although he never would have admitted it to anyone. But obviously, someone had fed him, clothed him, and provided a roof over his head, a car, and driving lessons ...

As he looked back over his life, Phil was gradually becoming aware that every act of "independence" and "achievement" on his part—getting a degree, landing a great job, flying all over the world—had actually been made possible by others, from those who paid his tuition to those who believed in him enough to take the risk of giving him his first job, to those with the training and experience to safely fly a jumbo jet across oceans.

Sure, he had had a small part in it all, but as he sat in the pew, still grey with ashes and utterly clueless as to what was going to happen next, he was realizing for the first time Mankind's dirty little secret: that every living, breathing individual was helplessly dependent; some were just allowed for a brief time to believe that they weren't. They were all like children running around the mall play area, doing their thing and oblivious to the watchful eyes of the adults that kept them safe.

At first to someone like Phil this was an extremely unsettling realization, but as he gradually began to let go of his pride and accept the notion, it was as if a rosy glow on the horizon was announcing a new day, and he wondered if the revelation he was experiencing was actually the beginning of a new stage in his life, one of enlightenment rather than despair.

And he wondered why, at that moment, the Cross that stood steadily before him seemed like the one remaining sign of stability in the world. Sure, he was helpless, and as he now knew, always had been. But somewhere, Someone wasn't, and the fact that he was still alive made him dare to hope that that Someone just might care about him, might actually have been looking out for him all along.

CHAPTER TWENTY-FIVE

September 12, 2001, 7:30 AM, EDT

"Good mornin', boys!" Phil couldn't tell where the gentle voice was coming from that broke through the haze as sleep was leaving. He opened his eyes and tried to figure out whether he was fully awake or still dreaming. The hard wood he was lying on certainly wasn't his bed, and the condition of his hair, skin, and clothes made him more anxious than usual to hop in the shower. But he had a feeling that wasn't going to happen any time soon.

"Phil?" Phil looked around to see another ash-covered person with the voice of his friend Ben. "Man, you look like hell."

"Thanks, friend. So do you. Where are we?" he asked hoarsely.

"Apparently St. Paul's Church," came the sleepy reply.

"Oh yeah," said Phil. "And it's still standing?"

"Yeah. Can you believe it?" Ben walked over to a window and looked out.

"So what's going on out there?" Phil asked.

"No idea," said Ben. "Can't see much except rubble and ashes."

In spite of what had happened the day before, there seemed to be a calm in that place that defied explanation. Turning and examining all sides, they could see that not one windowpane had been broken.

This is crazy ... I must be dreami—still dream ... It can't be. Dreams don't go on for days. Maybe I'm losing my mind ...

Just then the lady appeared, her flowered dress somehow cleaner than the day before, carrying two very welcome gifts for each of them: wet washcloths for their faces and bottles of water for their parched throats. (Oddly, neither Phil nor Ben felt the least bit hungry.) A few moments later they were recognizable again. The lady's face was clean as well, and they could see her kind eyes and encouraging smile as she said, "Well, kids, we made it through the naht."

Ben summed up his thoughts in one word: "Unbelievable."

"Miraculous," the lady agreed. "Ah'd say Someone's lookin' out fer you two." The men exchanged glances, and Phil had a feeling he couldn't have described if he had wanted to. It was completely foreign to him, but he liked it. Part of him was still stubbornly resisting the loss of his dignity and thoughts of the night before about helplessness. That part of him was clinging to the notion of independence and self-sufficiency. But an ever-growing part of him was winning over—the part that recognized that independence and self-sufficiency were not only overrated, they had been an illusion all along. And as the new day dawned, he was ready to abandon the non-existent to explore the wonders of the reality he was on the brink of discovering. He felt utterly childlike, and that was OK for now.

"So ... what now?" Ben asked the lady.

"Ah'll show you where to go," she explained, unlocking the door. "There'll be people who can help you from there. You'll be fahn." She turned and looked at them eye-to-eye. "Just remember to be thankful," she admonished solemnly.

When they had finished their water, the lady took out a clean handkerchief and tied it over her nose and mouth. She then gave them each a clean handkerchief of their own, and they tied them onto their faces.

Standing on the threshold, Phil took one more look at the sanctuary, especially the Cross. He was oddly reluctant to leave, having found a security there he couldn't explain. He hoped that the feeling would go with him, at least until they reached safety. He was already getting apprehensive about going back out into the grey netherworld.

"Y'all ready?" the lady asked. The men nodded, and she opened the door to the next leg of their journey. "OK, follow me, boys." A thick layer of ash covered the ground, and rubble was everywhere. To the men's astonishment, a huge old tree had been uprooted just a few feet from the church. But it had not destroyed or even damaged the church. On the contrary, its gigantic root system towered over them like a giant shield, protecting the building from harm. The lady didn't seem surprised but continued to lead the way around the tree and up the street. Again she seemed to know exactly where to go, and again the two businessmen followed her without questioning.

CHAPTER TWENTY-SIX

September 11, 2001, 9:15 AM, EDT

Saundra gripped the handrail tightly to keep from slipping on the water that was flowing down the stairwell. She tried hard to stifle the sobs. After all, she was a Christian, and although it was becoming apparent that this was a life-threatening situation, she was not feeling afraid—at least not for herself.

What she was feeling was bitter disappointment, disappointment that the day was not going as she had hoped. When Phil O'Brien had told her that he was meeting his nephew and his new bride, she had hoped—she had to admit, she had expected—that she would see her many prayers for her boss begin to be answered. She knew from the little Phil had told her that his brother was a dedicated evangelical pastor, and that all three of his children were also "born again." Saundra knew that they had what Phil very badly needed, and yet he rarely saw them. As the day of the visit approached, her prayers for her boss had intensified, and though she had tried not to set herself up for a disappointment, she couldn't help anticipating his making a life-changing decision sometime in the near future. In fact, she had hoped and prayed for it with all her heart, for reasons known only to her and her Lord.

She didn't know whether or not Phil had the same feelings for her that she had for him. It seemed sometimes that the attraction was mutual. But she knew for certain that unless he was a believer—a follower—of her God, there was no future for them as a couple. They would be like the "unequally yoked" oxen, pulling in separate directions, eternally frustrated. So she had prayed. And hoped.

Saundra knew deep down that it was foolish to hang one's hopes on a single meeting over breakfast, and yet ...

So close! she thought as they reached the SkyLobby. *He was on his way to meet them, and who even knows where they are now? And what if he doesn't even live to the end of the day?*

As if to accentuate her fears, the Tower gave an eerie groan, and Saundra could feel the floor tilting.

"It's falling over! We're going to die!"—*and go our separate ways! I'll never see him again!*

"Maybe so, but we'll die running!" Phil declared through clenched teeth. Grabbing her hand, he dragged her to the stairwell.

During the eternity they were making their way down, Saundra was now weeping, and it was all she could do to keep from collapsing on the stairs. The news that the South Tower had also been hit seemed to have drained what was left of her strength.

When at last they reached the ground floor, the scattered shards of glass, clouds of dirt and smoke, and the rain of flaming pieces of the Tower looked to Saundra like the Apocalypse.

The world is ending! she thought. *Not yet, Lord!* she prayed. *Please! He's not ready!*

Since with the falling debris there was obviously not going to be any exiting the building here, the refugees were herded down to the lower levels. Saundra was starting to get claustrophobic. She was thinking she would feel so much better if Phil would take her hand again, but then she realized he was no longer right behind her. She looked over her shoulder but could not see him. Her heart sank; would she ever see him again?

"Keep moving!" the firemen shouted to the people at the bottom of the escalator. Saundra started to move with the flow of the crowd, but soon decided that she couldn't leave without knowing where *he* was—physically *and* spiritually. Stepping aside, she stood scanning the faces of the people as they passed. She *had* to find him, if only to tell him one more time—more directly this time—what he needed to know before it was too late: that Jesus died for him, paid for his sins, and that whether Phil lived another five minutes or fifty years, he was promised eternal life, if he would just believe.

For what seemed like another eternity, she waited and watched but didn't see Phil or his friend. It then occurred to her that they may have somehow passed her and were now far ahead.

She hurried as quickly as the crowded conditions allowed and followed the streams of people up to the street.

The air was filled with fluttering papers, and Saundra became frustrated trying to find Phil through what resembled a tickertape parade.

Suddenly the ground shook, and a sound like ten jumbo jets thundered overhead. Black clouds of dust and debris and large chunks of concrete began falling.

"JESUS!" Saundra cried instinctively. And even as she knew that she would probably meet Him soon, her last thoughts before losing consciousness were of Phil, her last prayer a plea for his salvation.

CHAPTER TWENTY-SEVEN

September 11, 2001, 5:30 PM, CDT

The prayer vigil at Faith Chapel had begun as an emergency meeting of the church staff and had steadily grown throughout the day, as retired members came in, as well as stay-at-home moms with their infants, toddlers, and homeschooled children. Shannon and her friends had joined them after school, and shortly after 5:00 there was an influx of adults who came directly from work. People knelt at the altar, stood in small circles holding hands, or sat in pews with their arms around one another. Throughout the sanctuary prayers could be heard, mingled with sobs, and occasionally a group would break into singing softly "It Is Well With My Soul," or some other song of trust. As night fell, most went their separate ways, while some—mostly seasoned "prayer warriors" and homeschooled teens who had spent the bulk of their day helping with the little ones—stayed to pray through the night.

As the early morning rays of sunlight crept through the windows, people began flowing in again—people who had loved ones in New York City, people who knew people who did, or just people who knew the nation was badly in need of the hand of Providence and that prayer was the only answer.

Pastor Dan had been there the whole time. Upon hearing of the attack and witnessing the collapse of the buildings shortly after, he himself had collapsed in a heap at the altar, pleading with God for his son, his new daughter-in-law, and his brother. Mercifully, good news had already come from Sean and Liz, who had contacted him saying they were alive and safely in their hotel room. Although the weight was no longer unbearable, Dan was still heartsick thinking about his brother. Sean and Liz, of course, had no news to give him regarding Uncle Phil; now that it was the day after, still with no news, everyone feared the worst.

Still, Pastor Dan continued to pray intensely, as he had done from the moment he had received news of the attack.

"Lord, have mercy on my brother, please ... please ... wherever he is, send Your angels to keep him safe. Let him know You are there, that You are real, and that You care for him. Please, please don't let him leave this world without knowing You!"

Friends and family had joined him in praying specifically for Phil. Many had unbelieving loved ones of their own; they knew the heartache and could only imagine the agony of not knowing if one of those loved ones was even alive.

Colleen had been going through flashbacks of losing her own brother, Sean, who years ago had been in the wrong place at the wrong time. At the first news of the day she had panicked to think her son Sean might also have been taken from her just as suddenly. The call from him had alleviated those fears, but her empathy for her husband, who now feared losing his own brother, and concern for others in the congregation, together with the sheer horror of it all, left her emotionally drained. Several times during the night her strength would give out, and she would sleep soundly for an hour or two, her head on the shoulder of her husband, who didn't have the heart to move and awaken her.

Finally, at the sound of people coming in the next morning, she stirred. She was going to ask Dan if he'd received any news of Phil, but one look at his haggard face had told her "no." She put her arm around him and added her prayers to his.

"Lord, we trust You with Phil. We trust that one way or another, You and Your angels are with him."

It was almost noon on Wednesday when Dan's cell phone interrupted the flow of prayers. When he saw that it was a call from New York City, his heart stopped. He stepped into the corridor and with trembling hands fumbled to answer the call. Colleen waited in the pew, her prayers suddenly doubling in intensity.

When Dan reentered the sanctuary, she couldn't read the expression on his face. His hands were still trembling as he knelt back down next to her.

"Thank You, Jesus! Thank You!" he sobbed. Suddenly pulling himself together, he stood to address the whole gathering.

"Excuse me, friends. As much as I hate to interrupt your prayers, I have some news," he announced in a voice that was still shaky. All eyes were on him. "My brother has been found ... " The congregation held its breath. " ... alive ... " There was a murmur of approval. " ... and well." As he said the final words, his voice broke, and with a collective sigh of relief the devoted prayer warriors shared a moment of "amens" and hugs before getting back to business.

Dan and Colleen, however, lingered in an embrace, sobbing in gratitude.

CHAPTER TWENTY-EIGHT

September 19, 2001, 6:45 PM, CDT

The familiar surroundings of Faith Chapel made it feel as though Liz and Sean had never left. The emotional roller-coaster of the preceding weeks seemed like a dream, both absurd and surreal. The weeks of stress before the wedding, a week of fretting over the details of the event all turning out "just right," (and finding that God did, indeed, have everything under control) had been followed by a major disaster close enough to make Liz realize how ridiculously trivial her worries had been. She had given up trying to fathom why the God who provided her with wildflowers, perfect weather, and a rainbow for their special day had seemingly stood by as evil monsters flew airplanes into buildings, devastating thousands. The guilt of having been spared while multitudes perished haunted her incessantly, especially knowing that for so many families the nightmare was only beginning and would go on for months, years, lifetimes, and there was very little she could do.

The Wednesday after they had returned to Chicago, Liz was doing the one small thing she could to help.

"Hi Miss Danfiel—I mean, *Mrs. Obrien!*" the 14-year-old stammered as she arrived to volunteer in the nursery.

"Hey, I'm still getting used to the title myself, Chelsea," Liz laughed. "How about just calling me 'Liz'?" The teenager already seemed so much older than when Liz had first met her a little over a year ago. Liz, on the other hand, still felt so much like a teen herself that even the title "Miss" had thrown her off, let alone "Mrs."

"So where's Mrs. Tangel?" Chelsea wanted to know. "Is she running late?"

"No, I'm subbing for her tonight. She's gone to a memorial service," Liz answered, and even as she said it, there was that familiar twinge of pain at the thought of why the nursery lady was absent.

"Oh, that's right! I heard she had some family that was in the 9-11 thing," said Chelsea, wide-eyed. "Weren't they on one of the planes?"

"Something like that ... " Liz murmured, not really wanting to get her mind on that painful subject again, although she knew Chelsea was at an age where life was nothing without drama.

"I heard you and your husband were in New York City that day! Did you see the planes hit?"

"No, we were in a different part of town at the time," said Liz vaguely.

"Oh, I'm *so* glad you're OK!" Chelsea exclaimed passionately. Liz smiled at the girl's apparent sincerity.

"Thanks, Chelsea. Yeah, God was really good to us." She knew Chelsea would probably relish all the details of their adventure, but she could already see some parents coming down the hall with their toddlers, and she needed to focus on her duties.

"Can you get out the toys and get the kids occupied while I sign them in?" she asked, effectively changing the subject.

"Sure," said Chelsea, smiling at the first little one to come through the half-door and taking her hand. "Hi Kelly! Hey, that's a pretty hair bow you've got!"

As the toddlers were being dropped off by their parents, Liz filled out a "claim ticket" for each child's parents and a nametag to stick on each child's back. Soon the brightly painted room was teeming with energetic toddlers, whose chief goal in life was to explore anything and everything as fast and as thoroughly as possible. For the first fifteen minutes they pulled virtually every toy off the shelves, and some stacked multicolored blocks while others ran toy cars through the rice in a shallow wooden box, forming little rice highways and tunnels. Although the events of 9-11 still seemed dreamlike, it also seemed strangely odd to Liz that these children were so unconcerned about the state of their nation and the world; she almost felt as if there were two realities, and she didn't quite fit into either of them

She began to feel more sense of normalcy, however, when she got out her guitar and began singing with the children. Music had always been therapeutic for her, and it was her "default" activity when not knowing what else to do. Soon she was enjoying the children's exuberant responses, as some would try to sing along, some would reach out to pluck the strings themselves, while others simply bounced in place, clapping their chubby hands with glee. Still others paid no attention but managed to amuse themselves elsewhere in the room, under Chelsea's supervision.

These were Mary Ann Tangel's "little lambs," and a picture on the wall said it all, the picture that Liz's attention was repeatedly drawn to that night.

It was a familiar rendering of Jesus, the Good Shepherd, carrying a lamb on His shoulders. Something about the tenderness in His eyes made Liz feel like crying. At first she didn't know why, other than the fact that recently she was responding to things with even more emotion than she had before.

But somewhere in the midst of the little voices singing their songs of childlike faith, the dream from the morning of 9-11, the dream that had been coming back to her in bits and pieces, suddenly came together in its entirety like an emotional avalanche. In that moment she remembered every detail, as if she had just awakened.

The jagged rocks on the mountain shone white in the sunlight. The grass was a rich green, the sky a gorgeous azure. Tiny wildflowers dotted the hillside where a rough path, barely visible, wound its way up to where Liz lay enjoying the day. An eagle soared above her, casting a fleeting shadow across her face. She closed her eyes and sighed with pleasure.

Moments later she sensed another shadow, larger and darker, that brought with it a sudden chill. Opening her eyes, she saw that dark clouds were gathering overhead, and at once she was able to make out the source of the sudden anxiety. Scarcely twenty feet away, an enormous wolf stood frozen in place, its eyes locked with hers and its white fangs exposed ominously. A low growl came from its throat, and Liz was horrified to hear a second growl answer from the thicket behind her. She looked around in desperation for a place to hide— a tree to climb—anything.

Panic set in as Liz realized she was surrounded with no way of escape. The clouds that had rushed in out of nowhere gave a low rumble. The beast in the thicket stepped out into the open, and Liz saw that it was even larger than the first. Both wolves stood poised for the attack, the fur standing out on their backs. Liz was trembling uncontrollably as terror was fast giving way to despair.

Just then the huge figure of a man leaped between Liz and the wolves. His back was to her, but she could see that he was draped in a white tunic that was tied up at the waist to allow more movement. His limbs were tan and muscular, and his calloused hands gripped a long, heavy staff.

Without hesitation, he swung the staff in a wide arc, and the two wolves took a step back, intimidated. Both beasts snarled, but Liz could see that now they were the ones trembling. One of them lunged at the shepherd but was knocked to the ground in one blow. The other leaped from behind, only to be thrown aside when the man spun around.

Enraged, both of the monsters attacked at once, seizing his wrists in their vice-like jaws. The shepherd shook them off, but by now blood was pouring from his hands.

With determination, he continued to swing the staff as if it were a giant sword, driving both assailants back until they fled into the darkness, yelping like wounded puppies.

Suddenly Liz noticed stars in the darkened sky, and she felt an overwhelming drowsiness. She wanted to speak to her defender, to thank him, but the terror had drained her both physically and emotionally, and she found that all she could do was collapse into the lush grass and sink into a deep sleep.

The last thing she remembered was being scooped up in strong arms and held close to the warm body of her rescuer. A massive, calloused hand stroked her cheek and a gentle voice whispered, "It's all right. Go to sleep, little lamb. You're safe."

Peace. The picture on the wall said it all. Except in her dream the Shepherd's hands had been covered with wounds from the wolves He had fought off to save her. Clearly the dream had explained what the Lord was doing for her, even before it happened. What it didn't explain was …

Why? she thought. *So many people—thousands of people—good people—gone. Why were we spared?*

Later, as she told the children a Bible story, one little cherub climbed up onto her lap and snuggled up to her. Again Liz felt the tears welling up, and she put her arm around the tiny girl. She glanced up at the picture and felt like a child herself, snuggled on her Shepherd's lap, safe, warm, and secure.

Why me? she wondered again, overwhelmed with gratitude.

After the service Liz opened the top half of the door, and the parents lined up to retrieve their children. Each one handed Liz a claim ticket, and Liz and Chelsea said goodbye to the toddlers one by one until the last one had left. Chelsea's friends appeared at the door, and the next thing Liz knew, she was alone with the mess. She sighed.

"Excuse me, I'm here to pick up Lizzie O'Brien," said a familiar voice at the door, and the familiar face that went with it gave Liz a playful grin.

"I need your claim ticket," Liz demanded sternly.

"No problem," said Sean, holding out his left hand. "I think you'll find this ring matches the one she has."

"So it does!" Liz exclaimed. "That means you're the lucky guy that gets to help me clean up," she added, flinging open the bottom half of the door.

"No problem," said Sean again. He grasped his crutches and hobbled in.

Liz gathered up the toys and put them back on the shelves while Sean slowly made his way around the tables picking up crayons.

Liz was doing the last bit of sweeping up around the rice box when she noticed Sean staring pensively at the same picture that had captured her attention earlier. He had an awestruck look on his face, and Liz questioned whether or not she should interrupt his epiphany to ask him what he was thinking.

She quietly put away the sweeper and came over to where Sean was still gazing at the image of the Good Shepherd. She put her arm around him, and he returned the gesture. For a moment neither said a word.

"I don't think I ever told you how I tore those ligaments in Central Park."

"You didn't really have a chance to. It kinda got overshadowed by … everything else that happened that day. I knew that you had fallen and twisted your knee. How many ways can that happen?"

"But I didn't tell you I was pushed."

"*Pushed?* You mean you were *attacked?!*"

"At first I thought that's what it was, but when I looked around I didn't see anybody, so I'm not sure *what* happened, really." Sean had a puzzled, faraway look on his face.

"How strange. … So either the person that pushed you disappeared in a hurry, or … "

Sean still hadn't taken his gaze off the Good Shepherd.

"I don't know," he said. "But whoever, whatever it was, He let it happen."

"I … I guess He did," said Liz, beginning to see what he was getting at.

"*He saved us,* Liz. If I hadn't been injured … " Liz shuddered at the thought of how close they had come to being among the casualties. Then she looked a little more closely and realized why this picture suddenly had so much significance to Sean.

The little lamb had a bandage around one leg.

CHAPTER TWENTY-NINE

In the midst of the South Manhattan wilderness of rubble and despair, St. Paul's was an oasis. In spite of the horrific, gloomy surrounding, the sun was shining on the little church, which had miraculously remained intact while buildings all around had crumbled like sandcastles at high tide; even the tombstones in the cemetery stood undamaged. A line of people was moving slowly past a row of tables, where volunteers doled out hot dogs, beans, water bottles, and encouragement.

Phil and Ben paused to take in the scene. As remarkable as the building's survival was, the unity of the people was even more striking. As much as September 11 had seen the worst of Mankind, the aftermath had brought out the best.

It was the first time they had seen St. Paul's since they had taken refuge there with the Southern lady a little over a month before. In fact, it was she they were coming to see. Though they didn't want to interfere with the work that was going on, they also didn't want to wait any longer to thank the woman who had brought them through their ordeal. Phil was carrying a bouquet of flowers they had purchased just before coming to Ground Zero.

They searched the faces of the volunteers, and though they saw traces of the kindness they had seen in her eyes and the gentleness they had remembered from her warm gestures, their rescuer could not be found.

"Maybe she's inside," Ben suggested. They made their way to the entrance, where a woman had stepped out for a breath of fresh air. Seeing the flowers, she gave them a sympathetic smile and held the door open for them.

Inside, the church looked dramatically different from the quiet scene they had left behind. The sanctuary was now teeming with activity. People were lighting candles and praying. Clergy and social workers were counseling the grieving. Some rescue workers slept in the pews, while others lay on tables, where chiropractors and massage therapists worked on their aches and pains. A podiatrist was treating a firefighter's burned feet. In the front of the sanctuary a guitarist played classical music that added to the unique atmosphere. Pictures of the departed were everywhere, along with love notes ("We miss you, Daddy!") and personal items of various kinds. Children's drawings for the firefighters and letters of sympathy from all over the world were displayed prominently. Memorabilia, such as a charred firefighter's helmet and small signs displaying information about each one gave parts of the room the look and feel of a museum or a war memorial.

Phil and Ben searched the faces for their savior, but again saw no one resembling the person that had taken them to safety.

"It may be her day off," Phil suggested. "Should we ask someone?"

"Couldn't hurt," was Ben's response. They spotted a man who appeared to be a janitor. He was mopping the foyer with the same mop they had seen the lady use to clean up the ashes that had followed them inside.

"Excuse us," Phil said. The man looked up questioningly. "We're looking for a lady that works here. She's about fifty-ish … light brown hair … "

"Nice," Ben added. "Friendly. And she has a Southern accent. Do you know if she's here today?" The man thought a moment.

"I don't know anyone who works here that fits that description," he said apologetically. "You sure she works here?"

"Well, she had a key to the building, so we assumed she did," Ben said.

The custodian looked surprised and puzzled. "I'm the only janitor here today. We have some ladies on staff, but I know all of them. Nobody here with a Southern accent." He seemed amused at the notion. "Those flowers for her?"

"Yes," said Phil. "We escaped the North Tower on 9-11, and she brought us here to get us out of the cloud of ash. She pretty much saved our lives … " He stopped when he saw the confused look on the worker's face. The conversation came to a grinding halt. Finally, the custodian spoke.

"Son, you couldn't have been here," he said gravely. "Nobody was here that day, The place was locked up."

Now it was Phil and Ben's turn to be confused. The janitor was looking at them suspiciously, as if trying to discern whether this was a strange joke, or these were just two very confused men. For a moment no one said anything.

The awkwardness escalated quickly, until Phil said, "Well, thanks for your time. We'll let you get back to your work." They quickly left the uncomfortable scene and wandered through the memorabilia, reading the words on the signs without processing any of them. At a table paying tribute to the fallen firefighters, Phil laid down the flowers and headed for the door with Ben close behind him.

Once they were off the church property, Phil turned to his friend.

"Ben, I don't know what all that was about, but I think the less we say about it, the better."

Ben agreed wholeheartedly, and the two walked back to their cars without another word.

CHAPTER THIRTY

July 20, 2005

It was hard to believe that it had been almost four years since the Towers collapsed. Sometimes it seemed as though it had never happened at all—just a bad dream that was best forgotten. Other times it seemed disturbingly close, as though it had happened yesterday. Nightmares, the occasional news stories about terrorist activities, even the smell of something burning could to bring it all back—the horror, the grief, the fear. But the vivid memories also brought back the realization of what really mattered in a life too often cluttered with trivia. After all, for a brief time the nation had dropped the politics and celebrity gossip to join together and focus on what made America great in the first place: life, love, and liberty, family friendship, and faith.

So much had happened since then—Caroline's birth and the happy news that Liz was expecting again; Uncle Phil's move back to Chicago to attend Bible college (With his people skills and newfound passion for the Lord, he was a natural pastor.); Elaine and Rick's upcoming marriage ...

Liz stood on the crest of the sand dune, feeling the warm breeze play with her hair. The late afternoon sunlight sparkled off the water, and seagulls circled a family picnic, hoping for a handout. Children with "boogie boards" chased the waves and shouted to one another, while mothers sat on the beach towels chatting and ever counting the heads that bobbed in the water.

The resort town was the kind of setting where one dismissed all concerns about international politics and the disaster of the day. Newspapers were rarely seen among these people who had waited all year for a couple of carefree weeks in the sun. This vacation community seemed to exist completely isolated from the rest of the world and its troubles.

Liz was no doubt the only one at the beach thinking about the latest senseless act of violence, a bombing in London's subway. Although the attack had occurred thousands of miles away and nearly two weeks earlier, the newscaster's brief reference to the incident had set the tone for the rest of Liz's day—and beyond.

Her eyes were on the lake, but her mind was on the people still terrorized by the bombing and grief-stricken over lost loved ones. As flashbacks of 9-11 played in her mind, she could relate to what they were experiencing. She wished she could do something about it but felt helpless. She knew the best thing she could do was pray—but how? Yes, pray for the people, for God's presence to be felt, but she wanted to know how to pray that these things wouldn't happen in the first place. In this war with no borders, no uniforms, and enemies that could not be identified, how does one pray? For whom does one pray? What city, what country needed protection next? Liz started the only way she could think of.

"Lord, help me to pray." And she drew a blank. What good would it do to try to pray when so clueless?—"God, whoever is planning whatever for wherever … "?

She remembered something Sean's father had said about the most effective prayers: they were *specific*. Making general, vague requests like "God bless America," he said, was comparable to firing a shotgun into the air and hoping to hit something. But a *specific* prayer was more like a well-aimed rifle. And the most specific prayer was as powerful as a laser beam that could cut through steel!

"So how do I get specific about this?" she asked, feeling pretty power*less* at the moment. "I have no idea … I wouldn't even know how to narrow it down … " She sat in the sand, closed her eyes, and waited for some kind of answer—a leading, a thought—the voice of common sense?

Pray against what they have planned for today.

Of course. That narrows it down … a little.

Liz also remembered something about starting prayer with "adoration"—Christianese for acknowledging who the Lord is and the pray-er's need for Him and dependence on Him.

No problem there!

"Lord, we have enemies we can't see, but You see everything." It comforted Liz to think that the God Who loved her could see everything in the universe at once, including …

"They have plans we don't know about, but You know everything."

… and knowing that when human efforts fail …

"They have done things we couldn't stop, but You can do anything."

How encouraging to know that He was the …

"All-seeing, all-knowing, all-powerful God … " *OK, Liz, get to the point.* "I pray that no terrorist plans could be carried out anywhere in the world today."

As Liz watched the children playing in the waves, her thoughts went to children on the other side of the world, just as young, as innocent, but being brainwashed to think that the greatest thing they could do was commit suicide for their cause—and who were headed for a Christ-less eternity if they carried it out.

Suddenly for the first time she felt concern and compassion for the misguided souls who had hijacked the planes and caused so much misery. They were in misery now—in hell—and would be for all eternity, because they had believed a lie from their teachers, who had bought into the lies of *their* teachers, who had ultimately believed the "father of all lies."

The words of Jesus came to her: *"Love your enemies … pray for them … "*

"Lord, I pray for suicide bombers" … *so convinced* … "Please plant enough doubt in their minds to make them hesitate, and enough fear in their hearts to change their minds. Reveal to them that You are a God of love. Help them to renounce their hatred and embrace Your mercy."

OK, that prayer felt right. Still, God was a God that granted free will, and undoubtedly there would be those who would reject His offer of grace and cling to their hatred, who would continue to plot violence against innocent people all over the world … *all over the world.* Before she could feel overwhelmed, Liz reminded herself to narrow it down to one day.

"OK, Lord, regarding those people who have set their minds on evil and aren't going to repent … may their communications fail—let their computers crash, their cell phones disconnect—may their transportation break down, their calculations be wrong, their timing be off, their weapons malfunction, and their bombs be duds!" *(Wow, where did that come from?)* "Throw their camp into confusion, and foil every one of their plans today … "

This felt right, too. She wasn't praying against *them,* she was praying against their *evil intentions.*

" … that they may realize that You are the true and living God, and that even then some of them might be saved."

And their intended victims. Who were they? Liz didn't have a clue, but she knew Who did know them, every last one.

"Lord, I lift up every person who is a target of terrorists today, anywhere in the world. Lord, You know who they are. Please shield them from all harm."

Suddenly Liz realized that these people might not necessarily be right with God, either.

" … especially the ones who aren't ready to meet You face to face yet. Help them to know it was You that saved them, and that they owe You their lives, so they will spend the rest of their days serving and honoring You."

Liz found herself praying for heads of state all over the world—that those who knew God would be given wisdom, guidance, and the courage to do the right thing. She prayed for the ones who didn't know Him yet, that their minds would be open to His voice, and for those who were defiant, that they would have a change of heart or be replaced by someone who loved God.

She prayed for protection for those whose job it was to protect others—members of the military, intelligence, security, and law enforcement. She prayed at length for their protection and guidance, that they would each be in the right place at the right time, that they would see, hear, understand, and do what was needed. She prayed for them to have discernment beyond their natural human abilities and supernatural protection and boldness as they confronted evil.

She even prayed for any civilians God might be raising up to be involved in the War on Terror.

At the end of her prayer Liz felt drained but glad she had prayed, sensing that she had received divine direction somehow. Considering she had started out feeling inadequate and completely bewildered, once she was willing, there had turned out to be plenty of specific things she could pray for after all. And she knew God was perfectly capable of filling in the blanks. She had also felt a certain urgency in her prayers. She didn't know why, but it occurred to her that had she known what was being planned for the World Trade Center that September day, she would have prayed as long and as hard as it took to stop it. So, what did those elusive enemies have planned for *today?*

Her thoughts were interrupted by a beach ball flying in her direction. She caught it and flung it back to the children, who sang out "thaank yoou!" in unison and ran back into the water.

The contrast of immediate "reality" to her heavy thoughts and, for all she knew, a runaway imagination made her chide herself for her own sense of importance in a world of superpowers, rogue nations, and warfare someone like her could understand little or nothing about.

"Well, Lord, You know I mean well," she said sheepishly. "And I do love You," she added with a sigh and headed back to her parents' cottage to take Caroline so "Grammy" (Rachel) could start supper.

CHAPTER THIRTY-ONE

The story seemed to jump off the front page as Liz walked past the news stand at the party store. She stopped in her tracks, turned around, and picked up a paper.

Again it was London; again there had been bombs—this time four of them. But this time none of them had harmed anyone.

Liz bought a paper and took it out to the car with the donuts for Sean, who was just finishing filling the gas tank.

"Sean, did you see this story?" she asked as they were driving back to the cottage. "Four more bombs in London, but they were duds."

"All four? Wow, praise God," said Sean. "That's amazing."

"You wanna hear something else that's pretty amazing ... or at least a heckuva coincidence ... I was praying about that just yesterday."

"How?" asked Sean. "I mean, how did you know what to pray?"

"Well, I didn't know exactly, but I felt led to pray that if there were terrorists anywhere in the world that were planning something for that day that their plans would be stopped. Among other things, I prayed their bombs would be duds and their intended victims kept safe from harm."

"That's ... pretty specific, actually." Sean glanced over at the headlines. "And here's your specific answer," he added, somewhat awestruck. Sean had learned in the past not to question or make fun of Liz's "coincidences."

"I didn't know what was going on, but it's like God knew, and He filled in the blanks."

"Well, He does know ... "

"He's the *only* One Who knows, really. I mean, the War on Terror is a whole new type of war."

"Sure is. It's pretty scary to think that these guys could be anyone, anywhere. How in the world can anyone—people, armies, governments—stop them?"

"They *can't*," Liz insisted, as the proverbial light bulb was getting brighter. "That's why we need to fight them by going to the Only One who knows where they are and what they're up to."

"Good point. So, if enough people who believed in the power of prayer prayed ... !" Sean was catching the vision.

"—*every day,* it could really make a difference!"

"What hope do we have otherwise?" Sean concluded. Liz was sensing a "calling," at least for that day.

"Will you pray with me?" she asked as they pulled in the driveway. Sean turned off the engine and took her hand.

"Sure, hon. Why don't you just pray the way you did yesterday, and I'll 'amen' it," which was Sean's way of saying he'd be in agreement.

So they bowed their heads and prayed to the all-seeing, all-knowing, all-powerful God.

And inside the cottage George and Rachel wondered why it was taking so long for the kids to get a few donuts in town.

CHAPTER THIRTY-TWO

For what turned out to be years, Liz prayed daily, "standing in the gap" against terrorist activity, and occasionally when sharing her vision she would find someone else willing to commit to praying daily. One day she was sent a copy of the newsletter from a large church with a familiar prayer on the front page. At the top of the page were the words, "Warriors' Prayer." Liz smiled at the byline "Author Unknown" and prayed that God was raising up an army. She knew she didn't understand much about prayer, but it did seem that the more people were praying about something, the stronger those prayers were.

And she saw answers, such as a foiled hijacking that was allegedly planned to be "bigger than 9-11." It had been stopped at the eleventh hour, because a certain woman—an ordinary citizen—had thought her neighbors were acting suspiciously and had alerted the authorities. Other terrorist plans were stopped in their inception and suspects arrested. One day a friend told Liz about a piece she had seen on TV about a would-be suicide bomber who had been caught and had become a Christian in prison. And on Christmas Day, 2009, in spite of all the security, a young man managed to get materials onto a packed international flight and assemble a bomb, but the bomb failed. Another bomb failed in Times Square, and again numerous lives were spared.

Other times Liz would hear of a terrorist attack that took lives somewhere in the world and would realize that the day before she had forgotten to pray, or had started to pray after going to bed and fallen asleep. Not that she had any illusions about being the savior of Mankind, but if she and a handful of others were "standing in the gap," they needed to be diligent—which meant that praying for fellow warriors had to become part of her daily prayers, too. Otherwise, she figured, if the spiritual forces of darkness could manage to distract each of them all on the same day, the gap would be opened and evil allowed to break through. So her "warrior's prayer" became a priority for Liz. Even on days when out of busy-ness or distraction she didn't pray anything else, she would be sure to pray that one prayer.

If she ever felt her fervency waning, it only took a moment to get it back. The memory of what had happened that third day of her honeymoon was so imbedded in her heart and soul that she was committed to doing whatever an ordinary woman could do to see that no one would have to experience that kind of nightmare again for a long, long time.

EPILOGUE

Prayer could well be the most powerful force in the universe, and perhaps the only force that can be used effectively against an unseen, unidentified enemy that is not afraid to die in the process of killing others.

If you wish to join the spiritual warriors that are fighting evil on their knees, the following is the prayer that has been prayed daily since 2005. Whether you use the exact words or your own, you will be part of a mighty army. Only eternity will tell how far-reaching your prayers have been, how many souls were saved, and the impact you have made on history.

God bless you!

—Ann Aschauer

THE WARRIOR'S PRAYER

Father in Heaven, we come to You acknowledging our utter dependence on You.

Today we have enemies we cannot see, but You see everything.
They have plans we do not know about, but You know everything.
They have done things we could not stop, but You can do anything.

All-seeing, all-knowing, all-powerful God, we pray that no terrorist plan could be successfully carried out this day, anywhere in the world.

We pray for any misguided souls scheduled to be suicide bombers this day. Plant enough doubt in their minds to make them hesitate, and enough fear in their hearts to change their minds. Reveal to them a way of escape, and give them the strength to take it. Let them know that you are a God of love, that they may renounce their hatred and embrace Your mercy. Open their minds and hearts to the truth of the gospel, and send them someone or something to present that truth in a way they will understand, that they may receive salvation and be transformed into powerful, effective, passionate, joyful, fearless witnesses for You. Use them to light up the darkest corners of the world and the hearts of men.

Lord, we acknowledge that You grant free will to all, and that there are those whose hearts are hardened and whose minds are set on evil. We pray that today their communications will fail, their computers crash, their cell phones disconnect, and their transportation break down; may their calculations be wrong, their timing be off, their weapons malfunction, and their bombs fail to detonate. We pray that You will throw the enemy's camp into confusion, that they may know only that You are the true and living God, that even then some of them might believe in You and be saved.

We pray for anyone, anywhere on the planet who is a target of terrorism, especially for those who are not ready to enter eternity. Shield them, protect and defend them, and make Yourself known to them, that they may commit the rest of their lives to trusting, serving, and honoring You.

We pray for those who are in positions of authority, for princes, presidents, and prime ministers. Give them the wisdom and courage to do Your will. May any who are willfully defying You be removed from their office and replaced by another who will seek You and do Your will.

We lift up those whose job it is to discern the identities and locations of terrorists: the Secret Service, the FBI, the CIA, and Homeland Security. We lift up all those serving in the Army, the Navy, the Air Force, the Marines, the Reserves, the Coast Guard, the National Guard, the Border Patrol, TSA and all security personnel, as well as the Police and all law enforcement agents. May each one of them be in the right place at the right time; may they see what they need to see, hear what they need to hear, understand what they need to understand, and do what they need to do. Give them discernment beyond their human abilities, and supernatural boldness and protection as they confront evil. If any enemies have infiltrated their ranks, may they be apprehended and rendered harmless, or even turned into allies. We pray also for any civilians who are being called to take part in the War on Terror; may they have the courage they need to fulfill their calling.

And may we all be diligent in prayer, knowing that ultimately we depend upon You for our safety and our lives.

In Jesus' precious Name, Amen

CPSIA information can be obtained
at www.ICGtesting.com
Printed in the USA
FSOW02n0126040517
33779FS